CHIHUAWOLF

A Tail of Mystery and Horror

CHARLEE GANNY

Illustrated by Nicola Slater

sourcebooks
jabberwocky

Copyright © 2011 by Charlee Ganny
Cover and internal illustrations © Nicola Slater
Cover and internal design © 2011 by Sourcebooks, Inc.
Cover design by Rose Audette

Sourcebooks and the colophon are registered trademarks of Sourcebooks, Inc.

All rights reserved. No part of this book may be reproduced in any form
or by any electronic or mechanical means including information storage
and retrieval systems—except in the case of brief quotations embodied in
critical articles or reviews—without permission in writing from its publisher,
Sourcebooks, Inc.

The characters and events portrayed in this book are fictitious or are used ficti-
tiously. Any similarity to real persons, living or dead, is purely coincidental and
not intended by the author.

Published by Sourcebooks Jabberwocky, an imprint of Sourcebooks, Inc.
P.O. Box 4410, Naperville, Illinois 60567-4410
(630) 961-3900
Fax: (630) 961-2168
www.jabberwockykids.com

Library of Congress Cataloging-in-Publication data is on file with the publisher.

Source of Production: Versa Press, East Peoria, Illinois, USA
Date of Production: August 2011
Run Number: 15887

Printed and bound in the United States of America.
VP 10 9 8 7 6 5 4 3 2 1

This book is dedicated to all my cherished animals,
but particularly to

Baby Kitty
1989–2011

the tiny orange cat everyone loved.

CHAPTER 1

Long, dark shadows stretched menacingly across the backyard. The clock on the Methodist Church tower struck 8 p.m. A high, eerie childlike voice broke the night's silence.

"Oh, poop!"

Paco the Chihuahua hung his head. A fat tear formed in his right eye, became a silver drop, ran down his little black nose, and dripped onto the lawn. "Pardon my language, Pewy," he apologized to a very fat skunk sitting on the grass. "But it's no use. I sound like a cat with its tail caught in the screen door."

Professor "Pewy" Pewmount put a paw up to his chin and thought for a moment. "I believe the problem is that

you're a tenor. Not your fault. It's your tiny size. Try again. Begin the howl way down in your belly. Think of your throat as a long pipe. Push the sound up and out. I think you can do it."

"You do, *mi amigo?*" Paco brightened. He respected the Professor's intelligence enormously. After all, the old skunk knew how to get the lid off every garbage can in town.

Paco threw his head back, inhaled deeply, concentrated, and let loose a howl. "Ahhhhooooooouuuuu."

Pewmount clapped. "Much better, my friend. Much better. You've definitely improved."

Paco shivered with excitement. "*Ah sí?* Do I sound like a werewolf? Do I? Do I?"

The skunk got down on all fours and prepared to leave. Tomorrow was a trash collection day. He needed to visit all the garbage cans on Elm Street yet tonight. "I have never heard a werewolf, and I hope I never do. But you now resemble that Boston terrier on the next block. Maybe you will sound like a beagle if you keep practicing."

"But that's not good enough! I must howl like a werewolf by the next full moon. I wish I weren't *muy poco*—much, much too little." The miniature dog lay down on the grass and put his head dejectedly on his front legs.

Professor Pewmount, who was so fat he waddled instead of walked, moved slowly away into the night.

"Never put your wishbone where your backbone ought to be. That's what my sainted mother used to tell me. You got yourself into this mess…"

Paco rose and shook himself. "And I've got to get myself out of it. I know. *Gracias* anyway, Pewy."

A girl's worried voice rang through the clear night air. "Paco! Sweetheart, where are you? Oh my little *Paquito*, where are you?"

Paco cringed. He hung back. He did not go bounding up to the back door. He got down on his belly and backed quietly under a Hosta plant. Peeking out through the broad leaves with one eye, he spied a flash of pink. Two feet in bunny slippers marched directly to his hiding place.

"There you are! You are a naughty boy not to come when I call you!" A ten-year-old girl with short brown hair reached down and scooped the small dog up into her arms.

Paco whimpered and squirmed. It wasn't that he didn't love Olivia. He adored her. But he knew what she wanted to do. He had seen the bottle of nail polish on the kitchen counter. No werewolf wore painted toenails. Other dogs would make fun of him. Worse, Natasha—that fine, silky Afghan hound he worshiped with all his heart—would know he was a fraud. She would realize he wasn't a werewolf. He was

3

merely a small dog who told big stories to try to win her affection.

He couldn't bear the thought. He squirmed desperately as Olivia carried him toward the house. White showed around his dark eyes. His whiskers vibrated with fear. But he could not escape. Olivia tightened her grip.

"What's the matter with you?" she scolded. She pushed through the back door and entered the kitchen. "Don't you want to look handsome for your play date tomorrow? You must have a bath, and look over there. I bought you blue nail polish!"

Blue? Paco tilted his head. His ears perked up. *That changed everything. Rock stars wore* blue *fingernails. Rock stars were cool, fierce, and* muy *popular.* He immediately felt better.

Paco did not give in to despair, even when he found himself knee-deep in warm water, lilac-scented shampoo cascading down his back. He still had a few days to transform himself into the terrifying creature sometimes called the great *lycanthrope*—the dreaded werewolf.

Paco shivered with delight at the thought of becoming that feared creature of myth and legend. He could do it. He would no longer be a member of the smallest dog breed in the world, a seven-pound Mexican short-hair who trembled at the slightest threat. His outside appearance would match what he was on the inside— big, mighty, and fearless. He would have long fangs and sharp claws. He would snarl, and everyone would run. He would be irresistible to the woman he loved.

The woman he loved. *Natasha*. Paco smiled to himself. Her name sounded like a rushing stream. *Natasha*. Her dog tags jingled when she swayed. *Natasha*. Her barking fell like soft music on his ears. *Natasha*. Paco's mood darkened. She called him a canine cannoli, a furry fajita, a miniature snoozer. He sighed.

He tasted the bitterness of the truth. He knew where he stood with her. Natasha didn't like puny little pooches. She only gave her heart to *perros grandes*—big dogs! Great Danes. German shepherds. St. Bernards. Rottweilers. Mighty mastiffs. And if they were bad dogs—dogs who dug huge holes in the yard, dogs who chewed up entire sofas, dogs who picked fights or stole bones or ran away for hours—Natasha liked them even better. Only the biggest, the baddest, the boldest leader of the pack became the beautiful Natasha's boyfriend.

Paco the Chihuahua, the *poquito*, the pipsqueak, could never win her—but maybe Paco the Werewolf would.

There were demons in the house. Norma-Jean and Little Annie looked like ordinary cats, one gray, one black, but Paco knew the truth. Nothing was ordinary about them. Those two possessed criminal minds. They stole his food. They took over his doggy bed.

They spent their days plotting new ways to torment him. And like wisps of smoke or transparent ghosts, they slipped away unseen and were never caught at their misdeeds.

Now, fresh from his bath, his nails barely dry and magnificently blue, Paco entered the living room, hoping to watch some television before he went to bed. He was halfway to his favorite spot on the recliner when he heard giggling. He tensed. He swiveled his head. He saw four glittering yellow eyes peering at him from under the sofa. His breath quickened. He turned to run. But not fast enough.

A gray paw snaked out, and a sharp pain shot through Paco's tail. He yelped and spun around to snap at the offender. No one was there. Another sharp pain stung his tail. He yelped louder and turned around again.

Norma-Jean sat directly in front of him with a huge smile on her face. "Catch me if you can, little guy," she smirked.

Little! The word made Paco mad. Once again, being *muy poco* was his problem.

Paco growled and curled his lips back to show his tiny white teeth. He sprang forward. Norma-Jean dashed away. But before Paco could give chase, a black blur—Little Annie—raced up and swiped him on the nose as she passed.

Paco yelped even louder.

He heard laughter. The two cats stood on the back

of the sofa, their arms around each other's shoulders, their bellies shaking with mirth. Norma-Jean looked down and taunted him. "What's the matter? Legs too short to catch us?"

The thought rushed into Paco's mind, *If only he were bigger, they wouldn't tease him. Just wait until he was a werewolf. He'd show those cats.*

Paco took a great leap and landed on the sofa cushions. His frantic barking echoed through the room. The two cats scrambled up the drapes and climbed onto the curtain rod. They clung to the brass bar and peered down at Paco. They each gave him a wink. Then they started mewing as if their little hearts were breaking.

A few seconds later, Olivia rushed into the room. She spotted the two cats, who were crying piteously from their high perch. She saw Paco bouncing up and down on the sofa, hoping to jump high enough to reach them.

"Paco! Bad dog!" she yelled. She dashed across the room to grab him.

Paco didn't hesitate. He flew off the sofa in a flash and scurried as fast as he could into the kitchen. His nails clicked against the ceramic tile. He slipped and he slid. He made it to the doggy door leading to the backyard and plunged headlong through it.

But before the flap closed behind him, he heard Olivia crooning, "You poor, poor kitties. Did that mean old doggy try to hurt you?"

Smarting with the sting of being tricked, Paco hopped down the back porch stairs. His head hanging in shame, he walked along the flagstone path into the yard. He felt like a total failure. How could he be a convincing werewolf if two cats could outwit him?

He sat down, putting his little furry behind on the cool stones. He gazed up at the sky. A white half moon sailed across the star-strewn heavens.

Sadness gripped Paco's soul. He leaned back his head and howled. "Ahhhhhoooouuuu!"

A moment passed, heavy with silence. Then, from far, far away came a howl much deeper and more menacing that his own. "AHHHHHOOOOOOOUUUUU."

Paco jumped up on his four miniature paws. His hair stood on end. He trembled from the tip of his black nose to the tip of his black tail. He stared into the gloom. He saw nothing. But he knew without a doubt that out there in the dark, dark night, something very big, dangerous, and scary roamed.

CHAPTER 2

A *new day brings new opportunities.*
A night's rest and a yummy breakfast—uninterrupted by Little Annie and Norma-Jean—restored Paco's bright outlook. And Olivia had dressed him carefully. His trendy polarized shades went perfectly with his red baseball cap. A blue-striped polo shirt matched his blue nail polish. He peeked into the hall mirror and knew he looked smashing.

As he and Olivia headed out the front door, the thought of seeing Natasha at his morning play date made him quiver in anticipation. Then a ride in the car, one of his favorite things to do, brought him moments of bliss. With his spirits soaring, he arrived at the backyard pool of Olivia's best friend, Sandy, whose formal name was Alejandro.

Daylight sparkled like diamonds on the blue water. Joy bubbled up in Paco's heart.

Sandy set out water bowls for the dogs and a cooler with fruit juice and bottles of water inside for everyone else. He waved hello. Olivia and Paco were the very first guests there.

Olivia unsnapped Paco's leash, and he took a deep breath of air that smelled faintly of chlorine. He used his back foot to adjust the strap holding his sunglasses in place behind his ears. Then he unrolled a yellow towel next to Olivia's chaise lounge and lay down. He put his paws behind his apple-shaped head and turned his face toward the sun. He hoped to catch some rays and work on his tan. From the beach towel next to his, Sandy's dog, Coco, an overweight chocolate Labrador retriever, rolled over onto her back, trying to scratch an itch near her shoulder. "You know, Paco, you shouldn't have told Natasha your real name was *El Lobo*, the wolf." She turned a soft brown eye toward her small friend. "If she can't love you for what you are, she won't love you if you pretend to be somebody else."

Paco furrowed his brow. "*Por qué?* I don't follow you."

"Because she'll love the make-believe image, not the real you." Coco kept her voice gentle. She thought

Paco was a splendid fellow. He didn't have to change even a whisker for *her*. "I like you just the way you are," she murmured.

Paco didn't hear her. He had already closed his eyes and fallen asleep.

Almost in the next breath, a flurry of sharp, annoying yips woke him up.

"B-Boy's here!" Coco jumped up and barked a greeting to the Jack Russell terrier who ran onto the diving board, spun around four or five times, bounced up and down, and then dove into the pool.

A brown and white head quickly bobbed to the surface, and the Jack paddled to the ladder and climbed out. He pranced right up to Paco and shook, spraying droplets of icy water on Paco and Olivia.

"Stop it, B-Boy!" Olivia squealed and scrambled to her feet. "Tommy!" she cried out to the lean, muscular boy with spiky red hair who followed the Jack Russell onto the diving board. "Your dog's getting me wet. Make him stop!"

Tommy grinned at her. "Cannonball!" he bellowed, sprinted to the end of the board and jumped. He hit the surface with a loud splash. A geyser of water shot ten feet up into the air. Paco saw what was coming and scooted under the chaise just in time, but buckets of water rained down on Olivia.

"Nooooooo!" Olivia cried. "My hair!" She grabbed a towel and frantically started drying off. She happened to glance at Sandy, who choked back a laugh but ended up with a goofy grin on his face. She stamped her bare feet. "Your friend Tommy has no manners. And you're no better." She glared at the olive-skinned boy who had been her very first friend in kindergarten.

"Aw, come on, Livy! Don't be mad. So you got wet. You've got a bathing suit on. Tommy's just having fun."

Just then, Tommy's head broke the surface of the water near the side of the pool where Olivia and Sandy were standing. His wet fingers gripped the edge. His cheeks bulged out. His eyes twinkled. He bobbed straight up like a porpoise at Sea World, pursed his lips, and sent a stream of water right at Olivia.

She danced back, but the spray hit her legs. "Ohhhh, that's so gross. Tommy Thompson, I hate you for that!" Of course, Olivia didn't really hate Tommy. In fact, she secretly liked him a lot.

In the meantime, B-Boy kept barking. He raced all the way around the pool, came back, and did a couple of backflips in front of Paco. Then he threw himself down flat on his stomach, stretched out his back legs, twisted his head around as far as it would go, and started biting at the fur on his shoulder. "A flea! I think I've got a flea!" He yelped between bites. "I can't stand it. It's awful. I'm upset. It's a terrible flea. I can't get him!"

B-Boy sprang to his feet to try a different position. He aimed his head at his tail, curved his body like a doughnut, and began to spin. Around and around he went, yapping frantically, chasing the imaginary flea. He went so fast he became a blur.

"Do you believe that crazy dog?" Paco's voice was heavy with disapproval as he watched B-Boy's antics. "He has no cool at all."

"He can't help it, Paco," Coco said. "He's a Jack Russell terrier. Everybody knows they're show-offs."

"B-Boy!" Paco yelled. "B-Boy! Yo! I need to ask you something."

B-Boy slowed his circling. He raised an eyebrow and looked at Paco. Then he stopped. He straightened his body out, shook himself from head to toe, seemed to think for a second, jumped up on one front leg, and balanced for a minute. Then he came down and grinned a wide doggy grin. "Hey hey hey Paco. *Cómo estás*— what's happenin', homie?"

Paco rolled his eyes. "*Estoy bien*. I'm great. I'm your best *homie* in the whole world. At least, I will be, if you found out what I asked you to."

"Oh man, you sure you want to do this thing?" B-Boy nervously marched in place. His pink tongue hung out and he began to pant.

"I *do,* if I *can*. That's what you were supposed to find out. Can't you hold still for a minute?"

B-Boy was now doing a handstand on his front paws. He dropped down on all fours again. "Sorry 'bout that. I got this rhythm in my head and I just have to dance. I gotta dance, dance, dance." He began bouncing up and down.

"B-BOY! *Alto!* Stop!" Paco, frustrated, raised his voice. "Did you get on Tommy's computer or not?"

B-Boy kept bouncing. "Sure, sure. He leaves it on 24/7, you know? No problem. He went to sleep and I went right to Google."

"And what did you find out?"

"About you becoming a werewolf?" Bounce. Bounce. Bounce.

"*Ay, caramba!* Of course about me becoming a werewolf! Can I or can't I?"

Suddenly B-Boy became very still. Worry wrinkles appeared in his forehead. "Paco, my man, I don't think you should be fooling around with something like this."

"I don't care what you think! I need to know. Can I turn into a werewolf?"

B-Boy cocked his head to one side. Then he cocked it to the other side. Then he looked Paco straight in the eye. "Yes."

Paco shook with excitement. "Tell me! Tell me how!"

"Weeeelll. It's not that simple. I found two ways you could do it." B-Boy paused and looked about as serious as a Jack Russell terrier can ever look.

Paco's impatience poured over him like an icy shower. His nerves tingled. His skin twitched beneath his shiny black fur. "What are they? Come on. Tell me!"

"One way is—" B-Boy paused and took a breath. Then he scratched his side with a back foot. "It's…It's…"

"B-Boy! Come on! Spit it out." Paco's voice became very high and shrill.

"It's sorta complicated! First you got to put on a belt made from the skin of a wolf. Then you smear a magic salve all over yourself. Then you recite poetry, some crazy stuff, you know?"

Dismay darkened the Chihuahua's face. "*Qué?* I can't do *that*. Where would I get the belt? Or the salve? Or find out what poem to recite?"

"Yeah, yeah!" B-Boy panted. "That's what I thought too. Too many details. But I found this other method. Another way to become a real werewolf."

"Can I do the other way?" Paco's eyes lit up again.

B-Boy shrugged. "Sure. Why not? It seemed simple."

Paco dared to hope. "You mean simple dumb? Or simple easy?"

"Easy. Easy as pie. All you have to do is drink rainwater from a werewolf's footprint."

Paco's eyes glittered. He quivered with excitement. He barked his high, sharp bark. "Drink rainwater? That's a no-brainer. I do that all the time. I can be a werewolf!" He gave B-Boy a high five. "*No problema!* I can be a werewolf!" He and B-Boy did a victory dance. Paco looked like a chicken scratching in the dirt, but he didn't care what he looked like. He was happy, happy, happy.

From behind him, Coco coughed. Paco didn't turn. She coughed again, louder. Paco kept dancing, scratching the ground, hopping up and down. He was wrapped up in the moment. He didn't hear her at all.

"Paco!" she finally yelled. "Paco, there *is* a problem!"

Paco spun around. "*Problema? Problema?* What problem?"

Coco's eyes became very soft and sympathetic. She hated to upset her friend. "Paco, you're not thinking this through. You can drink rainwater. Every dog can. But you have to drink it from a werewolf's footprint. Where are you going to find a werewolf? I don't think any live around here."

Paco stood very still. All his joy vanished. He thought, *Coco's right. Where can I find a werewolf?* Then a memory tugged at him. His face brightened. "Maybe one does live around here, Coco. I think I heard one last night."

"You did?"

"I think so. I don't know so. Anyway, I heard an awful howl. It sounded really mean. It must have been a werewolf."

Coco didn't want to argue with the little dog, but she hadn't heard anything the night before, and she possessed very good ears. "But you don't know it was a werewolf. It was probably a big dog. Or a coyote."

Coco sounded very certain. Paco's head drooped down; his eyes stared at the ground. "I guess you're right. It must have been a big dog."

Seeing the effect of her words, even though she spoke the truth, Coco felt terrible for crushing the Chihuahua's dreams. "Maybe it *was* a werewolf," she offered, her voice encouraging. "One of the wild creatures might know for sure what was howling last night. Why don't you ask that friend of yours, you know, that old skunk who lives near your backyard?"

Paco's ears stood up. His nose twitched. Hope returned like the bedroom light flicking on early in the morning. "Yes! I'll ask Professor Pewmount. Even if he didn't hear it, he knows all the forest dwellers. They may have seen or heard something. News travels fast among the wild ones. I bet it *was* a werewolf. That's a great idea, Co—"

He stopped in the middle of his sentence. A wonderful smell had reached his quivering little nose. His heart beat faster. His head swiveled. His eyes widened. There, waiting for her mistress to open the gate into the pool area, stood a regal Afghan hound. Her narrow snout was raised upward, her curly tail was held high, her long golden coat was shimmering like waterfalls of silk.

Natasha. The dog who had stolen his heart had arrived.

"Hi, Victoria!" Sandy yelled.

The pretty girl who held Natasha's bejeweled leash smiled. Her straight, waist-length blond hair matched her dog's silky coat almost exactly. Her silver flip-flops matched her silver tote bag. Her sunglasses glittered with rhinestones. She waved toward Sandy and Olivia with a turn of her hand like the queen of England greeting her subjects.

"HEY, VICTORIA!" Tommy ran up onto the diving board again. "WATCH THIS!" He hurried to the end of the board, gripped the edge with his toes, bounced, and then sprang high into the air. He curved backward and completed a half somersault. Then his long, lean body sliced into the water gracefully, barely making a ripple in the surface.

Victoria clapped. She called out when he surfaced, "You did a perfect half gainer, Tommy! I give you a ten."

Olivia also watched Tommy make his amazing dive. Her face filled with a painful longing when she saw him emerge from the pool and rush over to help Victoria with her beach bag.

Sandy, too, focused on Victoria. He began to smile in a silly, dreamy way, staring at the lovely girl who swayed like a willow as she gingerly stepped around the puddles on the patio tiles. "She's really amazing, isn't she?" he sighed.

"You bet! She came in second in the regional championships last year." Olivia pretended she didn't know who Sandy meant.

"Championships?" Sandy sounded confused. "Oh, you mean the dog. Yes, she's a good-looking animal. But Victoria is…" He released a long, slow breath. "But Victoria is *beautiful*."

CHAPTER 3

Natasha sat with great dignity in the shade of a beach umbrella. A drop of water would not dare to dampen her narrow feet. The wind would not attempt to tangle her well-groomed fur. After all, she carried a royal pedigree. She was a princess at the AKC.

She looked down her long nose at the Chihuahua's eager face. "I told you before, munchkin. I cannot be your girlfriend. You are not my type. You are merely a raisin in the Raisin Bran. The dot over the letter *i*. A postage stamp on a letter. In other words, little dog, you are much too small for me."

"But I can change!" Paco tried not to whine, but he could hear himself, and he clearly was.

"Change? I don't think so. I like take-charge dogs. Big, brawny canines who are sometimes very bad. You remember Bruno, that German shepherd who used to ride around in the back of a police car? Hmmm? Yes? He had a crush on me. He asked me to run away with him—"

"Run away! You wouldn't, would you?" Coco's voice cut in, filled with shock and disapproval.

Natasha sniffed. "Not really *run away*, the way *you* mean it. At least not for long. I might have sneaked out for a brief race through the park. But that isn't the point. The point is I liked him. Who knows where it would have led if he hadn't chased a squirrel on duty and gotten transferred to a different station..." She sighed. "But you, Paco, you are not big. You are not bad. And it makes no difference whether you call yourself Paco or El Lobo. A name doesn't matter, little *muchacho*."

Coco, who was not quite as tall as Natasha but many, many, many pounds heavier, got slowly to her feet from her spot on the beach towel. She liked everyone, but when Natasha hurt Paco like this, she thought about grabbing that silky ear and giving it a good shake. The chocolate Lab could not keep silent another second. She butted in again.

"That's not true! Names have a strange way of

creating their own destiny. On the inside Paco *is* El Lobo. He has the heart of a lion!"

Natasha laughed. "A dandelion, you mean."

Paco blinked away his tears. It wouldn't do to cry in front of Natasha. He had to be cool. He stood up on his hind legs to appear as tall as possible. He puffed out his chest. He slowly took off his sunglasses and hung them in the neck of his T-shirt. He leaned an elbow on the edge of the chaise. He *was* cool.

"*Niña*, baby," he murmured. "I *can* change. I will. At the next full moon. You'll see. I am El Lobo. The Wolf. I will be fierce and dangerous. I will be bigger than Bruno the German shepherd! I will be bigger than any dog you have ever seen because I—I am a werewolf!"

Natasha arched an eyebrow. "You will have to show me before I believe you."

"*Sí, claro!* Of course! I will show you in—" Paco mentally counted, and he wasn't so good at math, "in three, or maybe four, days." He smoothly took his sunglasses out of his shirt and put them back on. He made his voice as deep as he possibly could and said, "Then, *mi amor*, you *will* go out with me."

Natasha laughed a deep, throaty laugh. "If you become a werewolf in three or even four days, Mr. Cocktail Frankfurter, I will be your steady girl."

"Hey, Natasha. Hey! Hey!" B-Boy was completing a head spin. "Look at me!" He launched into another power move called a windmill. Then he stood up on his hind legs and popped and locked all the way to the edge of the pool. Taking a mighty leap backward, he somersaulted into the water. It was a full gainer.

"B-Boy, on the other hand—" Natasha drawled in a voice as silky as her coat, "B-Boy may be rather short, but he—*he* amuses me."

Paco couldn't help himself. He growled. Natasha clearly liked B-Boy better than him. That Jack Russell was nothing but a doggone showoff. He'd never dare to be El Lobo. But Paco was different. He would do anything, no matter how dangerous, to become a magnificent wolf king fit for a princess of the AKC—fit to become the dog of Natasha's dreams!

Several hours later and back home again, Paco sneaked out the doggy door as soon as the sun set. The backyard was silent and empty. Not even a sparrow chirped in the bushes. Not even a field mouse scurried through the flower bed.

Where is everybody tonight? Paco thought.

Impatient and anxious, he paced up and down the flagstone path, up and down, up and down. He waited for nearly five whole minutes, which seemed like hours to him, before he spotted the white, aged face of Professor Pewmount appearing from behind the rock wall at the far end of the garden.

The old skunk was moving unusually slowly. He took a step and paused. His nose twitched nervously, testing the night air. A rim of red encircled his dark eyes. His head swung back and forth. He peered into the distance, watching for any movement. When he was sure nothing stirred, he'd start forward again.

Paco didn't wait for the skunk to get closer. He ran as fast as he could up to Pewy.

The skunk stiffened with surprise. Something like fear widened his eyes.

Paco didn't notice. The little dog was too caught up in thinking about himself to see that his friend was worried or scared. Paco's body trembled with excitement. He started talking as fast as he could.

"Pewy, hi! Hi! You know what? I heard something terrible howling last night! But I don't know what it was. Did you hear anything? If you did, do you think it was a werewolf? And if you did, and I did, he couldn't be far away, right? But he wasn't close either. So what do you think?"

Then Paco shook from head to toe, as all Chihuahuas do. It doesn't mean they're scared. They shake because their feelings are too powerful to keep inside themselves. And what Paco felt right now was impatient.

Professor Pewmount's sainted mother always said, "If 'ifs' and 'buts' were candy and nuts, oh, what a party we'd have." It was nearly the first thing that came into the skunk's mind as he listened to Paco's excited questions. He scowled at the little dog. He cleared his throat. He took his time. He finally answered.

"Yes, I heard something howling last night. The wild creatures in the forest did too. And some of the wild ones, those with the very best noses, smelled something. *But nobody saw anything.* So we don't know what was howling."

Disappointment flitted over Paco for the briefest moment, like a batwing in front of the moon. Then he thought of something and brightened. "Pewy, you said some of the animals could smell something. What did it smell like?"

The skunk looked away. He didn't really want to answer.

"Pewy, *please.* I need to know. Tell me, *please, please.*" Paco whined, feeling nearly desperate.

The skunk sighed a deep, ancient sigh and spoke. "The early morning chattering of the woodland animals agreed that the scent was terrible. It wasn't a dog. It wasn't coyote. It could have been a wolf. Yet no wolves have lived in this land for over a hundred years. A werewolf, I must admit, was hmmmnn— errrr—mentioned—by, by, ahem, a squirrel. Or maybe two squirrels."

Paco's ears stood up. "What do you mean, *mentioned?* What did the squirrels say *exactly?*"

Pewy rubbed his nose. He was clearly nervous. "They said, 'Last night was a night when humans could not rest in their beds, nor birds in their nests, nor foxes in their dens, nor could the stars stop twisting in the heavens. And on such a night, the werewolf howls.' That's what they said. Word for word."

Paco shivered. His eyes got very big. "I'm scared, Pewy," he confessed.

"You should be afraid. We all are. Everyone agrees that the beast, werewolf or not, sounds very dangerous. He's new to the area, and surely he has come to eat us, not to make friends. The entire forest is on high alert. The red-tailed hawks and blue jays are taking the daytime watch. The bats and owls are keeping guard by night."

Paco squared his shoulders and straightened his tail. "Even though it's very scary, I still want to find this werewolf. After all, I don't have to fight him. I just have to drink rainwater from his footprint. Since he's not far away, where do you suppose I have to go to look for him?"

Pewy shook his head in disapproval. "You are very young and very foolish. *Muy bobo,* as you would say. No one should go looking for trouble."

"I have to! Natasha will never love me unless I change who I am." He began to whine again. It was a very bad habit of his. "Please tell me where the wild ones think the great beast is."

Professor Pewmount's mouth got tight, as if he really did not want to speak. But if he didn't, he knew the squirrels would tell Paco sooner or later. Squirrels can never keep secrets.

"They say the creature is to the north. A few miles. Near the peak they call Mount Diablo. As I just said, you are young and foolish. You will never listen to someone old and wise. But you should heed me and stay away from there."

Paco did not hear the wise skunk's warning. He merely heard what he wanted to hear. "Only a few miles? That's splendid. I can run there and back before Olivia knows I'm missing. You know the country better than anyone, Pewy. Which road do I take?"

Professor Pewmount turned to leave. His mind was troubled. He wondered if he should have withheld the truth and told Paco the howling was a coyote. Then again, his long life had taught him that lies were never a good idea.

"Which road, my little friend? Take the white road, of course." He began to wander away into the dark.

Paco's heart beat fast. He didn't quite understand. He called out, "Pewy! I thought you'd give me a route number, not a color. Why did you say 'of course the *white* road?'"

The skunk slowed and looked back. "You are not a forest creature, or you would know that. A white road reflects the moon and stars; it can be traveled by night."

"Of course!" Understanding fell upon Paco like grace.

"Yes, my friend, but the wild ones also know that

because a white road can be traveled in the darkness, it can easily lead you into places you would avoid in the light. Dangerous places. Foul lands. Perilous kingdoms. You must be very careful when you follow a white road."

"I will be! I promise. Thank you, Pewy."

The learned skunk had reached the far side of the yard by this time. He was nearly out of sight when he stopped. He seemed to be thinking about something. He turned around. He called out to Paco, "I would like you to do something for me if you go."

"Oh, I *am* going. Tell me what you want. I'll do it."

The skunk's voice came across the grass like the whistling of the wind. "Don't go alone."

CHAPTER 4

Paco didn't have to think twice, or even think at all, about who would go along the white road with him, travel beyond the boundaries of his hometown, and stay the course until he reached Mount Diablo. No matter how long the way or difficult the journey, Paco had one friend who would never turn him down.

That friend—more true, more loyal, more trustworthy than all the rest—was Coco. Labrador retrievers have kindness and helpfulness woven into the very fiber of their being. But Coco had an extra measure of both. Paco knew that. Sad to say, he took it for granted. He and Coco had been pups together. They had tugged on the same chew toy. They had munched on the same bone. Coco had even sat back and allowed Paco to eat out of her doggy bowl. For a lover of food, as Coco clearly was, sharing her precious dinner showed how deeply she cared for him.

Therefore, Professor Pewmount's request to "not go alone" was already taken care of, in Paco's mind at least. But the small dog remained outside in the soft gray dusk to think about something else. He stared off into the gathering darkness and put all his brain cells to work on a plan for slipping out of the house and finding the werewolf.

He thought about it long and hard, hoping to create something terribly clever. Then a cricket chirping in the grass distracted him, and he forgot what he was thinking about. He tried a second time to come up with a plan before swiveling his head to better hear the musical call of a tiny peeper toad in a tree. He lost his train of thought again. Finally, he concentrated very hard, and this time, not interrupted by anything, he came up with a brilliant idea.

Paco hopped onto all fours, pranced up and down for a moment, shook himself to make his dog tags jingle, and with a light heart, headed for the house. The corners of his mouth curled into a wide smile. Happiness made him bounce. He had taken the first step toward fulfilling his dream. And he knew, with absolute certainty and not a glimmer of doubt, that his plan would work.

An hour or two later, Olivia called out, "Paco, come see what Mommy and I got you at the mall!"

Olivia's cheeks glowed a pretty pink and her brown eyes shone with excitement. In one hand she held up a plastic shopping bag that she shook loudly like a baby's rattle.

From his place on the seat of the recliner, Paco sleepily open his eyes. Instead of leaping to the floor and running over to see what she had bought (and he wanted to know what was in the bag, he really did), he lazily turned over on his back, put all four legs in the air, and squeezed his eyes shut as tightly as he could.

Olivia stared in amazement at the unmoving dog. Paco loved presents. She had never seen him act this way before. She turned to her mother. "Do you think Paco's sick?"

Unnoticed by Olivia, Paco's forehead furrowed into a frown. *Oh no! I can't let her think I'm sick. She might take me to the vet!* He must to do something quickly. He did. He snored. The snore made his whiskers vibrate. He snored again, louder. His cheeks flapped, showing his gums.

"That's no sick dog." Mommy's voice was brisk and no-nonsense. "That's a dog enjoying a good sleep. He wore himself out at Sandy's pool today, that's all."

"I guess so…" Olivia wasn't convinced. She couldn't remember Paco swimming in the pool or running around like B-Boy. She did recall him barking a lot with the other dogs. But could barking wear a dog out?

Finally she shrugged. She thought about how Paco was only a little dog. A very little dog. He must be delicate and easily tired. Pity squeezed her heart.

Poor, dear, fragile Paco. Barking was all the exercise he could handle.

"It's already eight o'clock. Let him get a good night's rest. He'll be his old self again in the morning." Mommy steered Olivia out the door and snapped off the light behind them. The sound of them talking in the hallway reached Paco, who still pretended to be asleep and snored as much as he could.

"And you know what, Livy?"

"What, Mommy?"

"I'm pretty tired too. Let me run a bubble bath, get you into your pajamas, and we'll read a good book together before we go to bed. Would you like that?"

"Can we read the book about Mole and Ratty and Toad of Toad Hall?"

"Definitely. I never get tired of reading that one."

Paco heard them move away and start climbing the stairs. Olivia's fading voice drifted downward.

"Animals can't really talk, can they, Mommy?"

Mommy laughed. "Only in books, Livy. Only in books."

As soon as they left, Paco jumped up. He wasn't the slightest bit sleepy. Excitement hummed through him like a vibrating guitar string. He wanted to howl with happiness. He listened to Olivia and Mommy climb the stairs to the second floor. He heard the bath water running into the tub.

He leaped into action. He ran over to the couch and grabbed a throw pillow in his teeth. He carried it over to the recliner and put it where he slept. Then he ran back to the couch and retrieved the small afghan throw Grammie had knitted. Taking it back to the recliner, he covered the pillow, so that if anyone should glance into the dark room—and he didn't think anyone would—the bump on the chair cushion would look like a sleeping dog.

Paco felt pleased with himself. So far, so good.

Next, he walked quietly through the kitchen, making sure his nails didn't go click, click, click on the tiles. He squirmed out the doggy door, taking care that the flap closed gently, without a sound. He went down the steps, stopped for just a brief moment, then marched determinedly toward the far end of the yard where Pewmount had rambled away a few hours before.

Paco knew about the dirt path that zigzagged through the area where the grass was never cut.

All of a sudden, a rabbit scooted out of it, raced across the grass, and disappeared into the high, dense weeds. Paco tensed. Was something else in there?

He gathered his courage and entered the path. Darkness closed in around him. Taking careful steps, he followed the twisting path to a place hidden behind some raspberry bushes. Here, the stone wall around the backyard had crumbled. It made an escape route that led from the safety of home into the wide world beyond.

Paco stopped. All he needed to do now was follow his plan. He could go through this secret exit to the next block, where Coco lived, without going toward the front of the house, where someone might see him. It was a great plan.

But when he had thought it up, Paco had seen only the adventure and the fun. Now, as the small Chihuahua stood alone in the dark night, his heart thumped hard in his chest. He felt nervous. His feet didn't want to move.

Then Paco squared his shoulders and told himself that Pewmount, who was a very old skunk, often traveled this way. Timid bunnies and worried mice did too.

But Paco never traveled this way, and that made all the difference.

In fact, he had never left the yard before without being in Olivia's arms or dancing at the end of his leash. Suddenly the world felt very big and he felt...he felt...well, he felt very small.

Yet he would not give up. He reminded himself he had the heart of a lion. Coco had said so, hadn't she? He pushed past the raspberry brambles. He climbed up and over the tumbled-down stones of the old wall. He told himself it wasn't hard at all. He looked around.

A narrow, brick-paved alley led between the houses to Elm Street. Paco lifted his chin, took a deep breath, and wagged his tail. He'd be at Coco's house in no time. There was no reason to be scared.

At that very moment, a movement to his right made him turn quickly. A dark shape came up over the wall behind him. *Ay ay ay! Run!* his brain commanded.

But it was too late. A heavy weight landed on his back and pushed him flat to the ground.

Paco yelped in terror. His heart fluttered like a trapped butterfly.

Who had grabbed him in the dark?

"Gotcha!" a familiar voice yelled. A very familiar voice.

"Get off me, Norma-Jean!" Paco cried out with a muffled sound—muffled because a gray furry body sat on his head.

"Make me!" the cat laughed.

So Paco did. He nipped at whatever was closest and caught Norma-Jean's tail with his teeth.

"Ow! That hurts!" the cat complained and jumped off.

Paco scrambled to his feet and saw Little Annie picking her way down the stones to join her sister.

"Where do you think you're going?" the black cat asked.

"We saw you sneak out of the house," the gray cat added.

Not wanting to answer, Paco asked a question of his own. "What are *you* doing out here?"

Norma-Jean rubbed her face with a dainty gray paw. "We always go out at night. It's when cats prowl. We can see in the dark, you know."

"But dogs can't," Little Annie chimed in. "So what's the story, half-pint? We *know* you're up to something."

"No, I'm not!"

The two cats exchanged a look that said they didn't believe Paco, not even a little bit. Then they spoke in perfect unison. "Yes, you are!"

Little Annie continued, "If you won't tell us, we'll just follow you and find out for ourselves."

"You wouldn't!" Paco's voice became very high and tight.

"Oh yes, we would," Norma-Jean nodded.

"Try us," Little Annie chimed in.

Paco didn't know what to do. He couldn't think up a lie to tell them, not one they'd believe, anyway. He hung his head. He might as well tell the truth. "I'm going to find a werewolf so I can drink rainwater from its footprint and turn into one myself."

Little Annie rolled her eyes. "That is soooo pathetic. You can't even tell a convincing story."

Norma-Jean stared at Paco intently, understanding dropping on her like a hard rain. "I know exactly where you're going."

"You do?"

"You're sneaking out to see your girlfriend."

"I am?" Paco's voice became a squeak.

"Why didn't you just tell us? We'd be glad to help you."

"You bet we would," Little Annie agreed.

"*Por qué?* You're not even nice to me."

"Of course we're not nice to you. What fun would there be in that? But that doesn't mean we don't like you."

"You like me?"

"Well, sure. You're—you're—What am I trying to say?" Norma-Jean looked at Little Annie for help.

"You're *family*," Little Annie said.

Paco didn't know what to say. He didn't know if he could trust these two. He guessed it didn't matter. He didn't have a choice. "Well, thanks, I mean, thanks for the thought anyway. I'd better get going. I'll be back soon, not really late. Way before dawn."

"We'll be watching for you," Norma-Jean said.

"We'll leave a light on for you," Little Annie added.

Then the two cats hopped up onto the wall and disappeared over the other side.

I wonder what they're really planning to do? The

thought flew through Paco's mind and then winged away. He had other things to worry about. He looked down the dark alley, gathered up his courage, and took off at a run toward Elm Street.

CHAPTER 5

ven a difficult journey over the tallest mountains goes downhill half the time.

Getting into Coco's yard took no effort. Her family used an "invisible" underground electric fence to keep her from straying. Coco was so little inclined to wander that most of the time they forgot to put the shock collar on her. She stayed inside the boundaries anyway. She knew she wasn't supposed to go any farther, so she didn't. She was a good dog and never gave anyone a bit of trouble.

Therefore, without encountering either a fence or a wall, Paco scooted into Coco's backyard. He bounded up the back steps and cautiously put his nose into the doggy door. He sniffed and didn't smell anyone. He cocked his head and listened for footsteps or voices, and hearing neither, he hopped inside. It was as easy as pie.

Paco softly tiptoed to the edge of Coco's doggy bed in the kitchen. "Wake up," he whispered.

Startled, Coco let out a small yip before Paco put a paw to his lips. "Shhhh. It's just me."

Coco's eyes got very wide. "Paco! What are you doing here? It's still dark out. Is Olivia here too? Has something happened?"

"Shhhh. Keep your voice down. I'm here by myself."

"You are? But why?" Coco's heart leaped for joy. She was glad to see Paco, although it was very late at night and totally unexpected.

"I sneaked out of the house. I'm off to see the werewolf."

"You didn't! You're not!"

"I did. I am. And I need you to come with me. You will, won't you?"

"Of course I will, but—"

"But?"

"How long will it take to find the werewolf? I wouldn't want my family to wake up and find me gone. They'd be very worried."

"*No problema, muchacha bonita,*" Paco grinned. "We will follow the highway out of town to Mount Diablo. It's only a few miles. The whole trip won't take more than three hours, there and back again. Maybe four, if we have to hunt for a werewolf footprint. But even then, we'll be back before dawn."

Bonita! He called me pretty. That was Coco's first thought. Then she focused on the rest of what Paco had said. She frowned in concentration. "It's really quite a long way. More than just a few miles, I believe. We'll need to take my backpack. We'll need water if we have to run far. Maybe a snack too. We'll definitely need a flashlight. Dogs can't see in the dark, you know."

"I know that!" Paco felt more than a little put out. The cats had said the same thing. How dumb did everyone think he was? Then a funny, uncomfortable kind of feeling started wiggling around inside his chest. He had never even considered the idea of bringing food and water or a light. He worried that maybe he had forgotten something else important.

While Paco's worries grew, Coco padded over to the refrigerator. She took two bottles of water from a shelf and a pack of frankfurters from the deli drawer. She might get in trouble for stealing them, but she was willing to take a scolding. If she and Paco didn't eat them all, she'd put the remaining hot dogs back. Her family might not even notice any were gone.

After getting the food and water onto the floor, Coco pushed the supplies into her backpack, slipped her front paws through the straps, nudged it over her head, and hoisted it onto her back. Then she walked over to the coat-and-hat rack by the back door. She stood up on her hind legs to reach one of the pegs and carefully removed the headlamp Sandy wore when he walked her at night. By squirming about and rubbing on the floor, she managed to slip the elastic band over her own head.

The headlamp perched on her forehead like a frog on a lily pad. "You'll have to switch the light on for me,

Paco. But we won't need it until we get to the mountain. The highway will be well lit."

All the while, Paco had paced nervously back and forth. He kept glancing up at the clock on the microwave. "Are you all set, Coco? We need to get started. I want to be at the mountain by midnight."

"Just one more thing." Coco went over to the outlet where the invisible electric fence was plugged in. She carefully knocked the switch to *off* with her nose. Then she looked at Paco and asked, "Why do you want to be there by midnight?"

"Because midnight is a magic hour. If a werewolf is out there on the prowl, he'd be wandering then, don't you think?"

The two dogs trotted along the wide, white highway that led from town toward the hulking black object that filled the horizon—Mount Diablo. Only an occasional car whizzed past. Whenever one did approach, Coco insisted that they hide in the weeds beyond the berm of the road. This slowed down their progress quite a bit, but Coco said she didn't want a good Samaritan to stop, thinking they were lost. *Or something*, she murmured, not wanting to suggest that a *not*-so-good Samaritan might want to catch them and steal them.

Coco was wise beyond her years.

Yet as long as they ran along the highway, the two dogs, one big and brown, one small and black, made good progress and didn't get very tired. Fewer and fewer cars passed them. Pretty soon, only huge semis rumbled by on the wide, white interstate. Sometimes Paco glimpsed the faces of dogs peering out the truck windows as they rode along in the cabs. The big rigs seemed in too much of a hurry to even slow down. After a while, Coco and Paco didn't bother hiding from them and were able to travel faster.

The waxing moon rose. Since it would be full in just a few days, even dogs could see quite well in the bright moonlight. Paco's confidence grew. His plan was working just as he had imagined. Perhaps he hadn't forgotten anything else at all.

After trotting along for an hour or maybe a little longer, they reached the foothills in front of the great, dark mountain. Here, the highway suddenly turned sharply to the right, away from Mount Diablo. Two smaller roads continued toward the mountain, one heading toward the eastern side; one leading to the western side.

At this fork in the road, neither route was marked "Werewolf This Way."

But the dogs didn't hesitate long before deciding which one to take.

Why? Because only one of the roads was white.

CHAPTER 6

A t this fork in the road, the route that was paved with tar and asphalt twisted to the left into a murky forest and disappeared. The road that was made of crushed white quartz sparkled in the moonlight and led uphill through open fields.

"This has to be the way," Paco pointed to the uphill road. He was puffing a little bit since he had to take two steps to keep up with every one of Coco's.

Trotting along, and quite enjoying the outing with her very best friend in the whole world, Coco smiled. "Yes. And I don't even have to use the headlamp. We can see very well. But Paco—"

"What, Coco?" *Puff, puff, puff.*

"When was the last time it rained?"

"Rained?" *Puff, puff.* "The day before yesterday, I think. Livy always puts on my red rubber boots when it rains. *Sí*, it rained two days ago, I'm sure. *Por qué?*"

"Didn't you say that you have to drink rainwater out of the werewolf's footprint?"

"*Sí, sí*. I did." More puffing.

"What if we find a footprint and there's no rainwater in it?"

Paco slowed his pace. He caught his breath. Doubt attacked him like a swarm of mosquitoes.

Coco realized her friend had fallen behind. She turned around. "What's wrong?"

"I didn't think of that." Paco's mouth drooped in an unhappy frown. He stopped walking. "Maybe the footprints will be dry, and we've come all this way for nothing." He sat down on the side of the white road, his head hanging.

Coco looked up. No clouds stretched misty fingers across the heavens. The night sky was so clear she could see the face of the man in the moon on the bright lunar surface. "It's not going to rain tonight." She paused in thought for a moment. "But it did rain very hard two days ago. There's a chance some water might remain in a footprint."

"You think there could be?" Paco lifted his head. A small flicker of hope rekindled in his heart.

"Yes, I do think it's possible. We've come so far, we might as well find the footprints, even if they're dry."

"*Ay, caramba!* If they are dry, what's the use of finding them?" Paco's hopes dimmed again.

"When will the moon be full, Paco?"

"Not until this weekend."

"And you need to drink from the footprint before then, right? To turn into a werewolf?"

"*Sí.* That's what B-Boy said." Paco cocked his head to one side and looked at Coco.

"And it might rain before the weekend, right?"

"*Sí.* It might," he nodded.

"Then we have to try. If the footprints *are* dry, we go home. We wait for the rain, then come back."

"Come back? You mean do this again?" Paco thought about how hard it was to sneak out and how far they had walked and how tired he would be when he got back. "I won't—"

Coco's eyes flashed. "Paco! Do you think dreams come true just by giving one try and giving up?"

"I guess not."

"Then how many times should you try?"

Paco frowned. "I'm not sure."

"Neither am I, but I think you need to keep trying until you decide that maybe that dream isn't going to come true."

Paco listened very carefully and considered what Coco had said before he spoke. "If it's not going to come true, what do you do then, Coco?"

"You find a new dream, Paco. Maybe an even better dream. And you go after it."

The two friends walked uphill on the white road for another quarter of a mile. The way became steeper. Paco puffed a little harder. The fields disappeared too.

Instead of the open meadows, bushes now closed in from both sides. Trailing vines snaked into the road and tangled around the dogs' paws as they walked.

Paco didn't like them. They weren't friendly vines at all.

Then the white road led under an avenue of trees, whose arched branches created a black tunnel.

Paco stopped. "I can't see where the road is going, Coco."

"Me neither." Coco stopped too. She put her backpack on the ground. "Let's take a break. I could use a drink. Are you thirsty?"

Paco's mouth felt dry as sandpaper; his pink tongue hung out. "I am!"

Coco removed one of the water bottles from her pack. She pulled the top off with her teeth and tipped it so Paco could lap at the water dribbling out. Then he held it for her.

"I'm hungry. Let's split a hot dog," Coco suggested.

"Okay!" Paco felt hungry too.

Coco opened the pack. She gave half a frankfurter to Paco and gulped down the other half herself. With a little food in her stomach, she felt much better. She stood up and put on her backpack. "You'd better switch on my headlamp, Paco. We need to go."

Paco hopped over, stood up with his feet on Coco's shoulder, and managed to turn on the light. Coco swung its yellow beam toward the darkness under the trees. The white road lit up.

"The road doesn't look too bad with the light on." Coco smiled encouragingly.

"No, it doesn't," Paco agreed, but secretly he thought it looked a little scary.

Very soon, Coco thought the same thing.

The dogs had gone just a short way into the gloomy tunnel when they spotted the dark shapes of broken-down cars and old refrigerators lying in jumbled heaps between the trees. Coco's headlamp also lit up broken baby carriages, heaps of worn-out tires, piles of weathered boards with nails poking through, and stacks of shattered windows, their panes knocked out. Wickedly sharp glass shards littered the ground.

They had entered a place of broken things.

"I think we're in a junkyard," Coco said.

"It smells pretty bad too." Paco's nose twitched as he took a deep breath.

Coco slowed her pace. Her voice became a whisper. "What does it smell like, Paco? Not garbage."

Paco began to shake. A terrible suspicion poked him like a stone in his paw. "No, it's not garbage."

Coco sniffed loudly. "It's definitely something else. It smells stinky and terrible."

Paco took a long deep inhale. "It smells—" He inhaled again. "*Ay, ay ay!* It smells like hate and fear. And, and—" his voice began to tremble, "it smells *alive*."

Coco whispered. "Turn off my headlamp, Paco. Be quick now."

Paco rushed over, hopped up, and flipped the switch.

The light went out. The dark closed in swiftly. The two dogs standing side by side could barely see each other.

"Shhhh. Listen," Coco said.

Paco listened. He heard something moving. He heard footsteps. He heard the junk on the ground go clunk under something's feet. He heard snorts, not like any human made, but not like any animal either. He heard a low, deep growling. He heard whatever was making all the noises coming, slowly, surely, step by step, closer and closer.

Paco quivered from his head to his tail. He wanted to run. "Let's get out of here," he urged.

"Paco, go. Go now," Coco said. But she didn't turn to leave. Instead, she took off her backpack.

"What about you?" He would not go without her. That he would not do.

"I'll use the hot dogs to try to slow up the—the *thing*

50

that's coming. I'll toss them on the ground. Maybe it will eat them." *And not eat us,* she added under her breath.

"I'll wait for you," Paco insisted.

As Coco frantically tore open the frankfurter pack, she talked to her friend in a fierce whisper. "I can run much faster than you. You need to go first. Run, Paco! Run now!"

And Paco ran.

Without light to guide him, Paco hurtled downhill through a dark so inky and absolute that only the feeling of the crushed stones beneath his feet helped him stay on the road. A few times he strayed into the dirt or grass. He instantly corrected himself to get back on course. But every time that happened, fear nearly took away his senses. If he accidentally ran into the junkyard, he would be lost for good in that terrible place of danger and broken things.

Finally Paco rushed out from under the trees and into the moonlight. With the white road now brightly lit, he started to scoot down the hillside. Then he stopped. His whole body trembled. His little legs shook. But he straightened his spine and squared his shoulders. He reached deep inside himself to find courage. He turned and looked back. He needed to know if Coco was coming. What if she had run off the road and was lost?

Nothing moved on the road behind Paco. Coco wasn't there. Paco didn't hesitate. No matter how scared he was of the creature that might be the werewolf, no matter how terrified he was of being eaten, he started to run back uphill toward the darkness to find his friend.

At that very moment, Coco burst into the moonlight from the darkness under the trees.

"Run!" she shouted at Paco. "Run! He's coming!"

Paco had never felt a deeper joy than he felt the moment he saw Coco burst free from the unlit and evil place. With a lighter heart, he turned around and dashed along the white road toward the highway.

Soon Coco caught up with him. Together they ran, tongues hanging out, breath coming hard, feet churning as fast as they could move them.

From behind them came a terrible howling. The awful sound chilled Paco's blood. It made him quiver from his head to his tail, even while he hurtled headlong down the foothills of Mount Diablo.

Coco stayed by his side. The comfort of her next to him made him feel better. He didn't feel so afraid as long as she was there.

After a little while, the howling stopped. The night became still. The two dogs slowed down and their ears perked up.

Paco swiveled his head one way, then the other way. He concentrated hard. He heard nothing, no footsteps, no growling, no snorts.

"Maybe he turned back," Coco whispered.

"He must have," Paco grinned. "We got away! He didn't get us!"

Coco gave Paco a smile, but her eyes were filled with worry. She hoped the howling creature had turned back to the mountain, but she wasn't certain about it. "No he didn't get us. But—"

Paco looked at Coco intently. Something was wrong. "What's the matter?"

"I—I—got hurt. I cut my back foot. I ran off the road and stepped on glass from the broken windows."

"Is it bad?" Paco's heart gave a painful squeeze.

"I think it is," Coco said, then quickly added, "Don't worry, Paco. I'm okay. Now that we don't have to run, I can walk on three legs until we get home."

"It's all my fault!" Paco cried. "You're hurt because of me."

"The glass cut me, you didn't." Coco took a little hop, keeping one back paw lifted. "I wanted to come with you. Please don't blame yourself."

But Paco did. His head hung down. He pushed away the tears that wanted to fill his eyes. He swallowed the sob that wanted to stick in his throat. He must be brave now. Yet inside he felt awful. He vowed he'd never sneak out or do anything so foolish and dangerous ever again.

Slowly, ever so slowly, the two dogs traveled toward town along the wide, white highway. The moon finished its nightly track from the east to the west and disappeared. The stars glowed more brightly against the velvet black sky. The air became chill and damp with dew.

Sometimes Coco looked back toward the dark mountain. A few times she asked Paco to stop so she could listen. She never said if she saw or heard anything.

Once Paco glanced behind them and saw dark wet spots on the ground where they had just walked. "You're bleeding, Coco!" he cried. His voice grew heavy with fear. "We need to stop. You should sit down. Wait here. I'll run ahead and get help."

"No!" Coco cried out. "I can't stay here."

"Por qué, mi amiga?" Paco asked.

Coco didn't want to tell Paco the truth. Her ears were better than his. Her eyes were better too. She had seen something sneaking along behind them. She had heard the panting of a large animal. She had realized the creature hadn't given up at all. He was back there, keeping his distance. He wasn't trying to catch them. He was following them back to town. She didn't know why, but she knew for certain that he lurked out there in the dark.

Not wanting to frighten her friend, she didn't answer Paco's question. She only said, "I just can't stay here. I'll make it home, Paco. I will, if we take our time."

And so the two dogs continued on their journey. Coco would walk and hop, walk and hop. Then they would stop for a minute. They moved slower and slower.

The night waned. The hours passed. On the far horizon, the first pearly light of dawn made a band of gray against the inky sky. Coco whimpered a little, but the two dogs kept going.

Paco worried that they would never reach the pretty houses and neat lawns of the streets he knew. He asked Coco if she wanted to stop, to give up until somebody came looking for them.

"Never give up, Paco. Never, never, never. Remember that." And she hopped on.

Finally they arrived at the edge of town. Paco recognized some of the buildings. His spirits rose. They were getting close to home. They started down familiar streets.

First they passed the cozy cottage where B-Boy lived with Tommy. It sat silently behind some hedges; everyone inside was sleeping.

Next the two dogs came to the large house where Natasha lived. A light suddenly flickered on within it. A sharp, clear bark sounded.

Paco gasped. His heart raced. "Hurry if you can, Coco. Victoria's brother takes Natasha out early to run with him through the park. It must be nearly time."

They slipped past the house as fast as they could. Nobody saw them, but from inside Natasha barked again.

Although it took a very long time, they never gave up. The small black dog and the large brown one finally arrived in Coco's backyard.

Coco sighed and sat down. She looked very tired. She pulled her headlamp off. "I can't climb the stairs, Paco. Please take this inside for me and put it by the door. I left my backpack in the junkyard, but it really doesn't matter. All that matters is that I'm home."

Paco grabbed the headlamp and rushed through the doggy door. He dropped the headlamp under the coat rack, then he hurried back outside. He saw that Coco was lying down. She wasn't moving.

Ay Dios mio! Fear gripped Paco. He sprinted over to her. "Coco! Talk to me!"

She raised her head a little and looked up at him. "Go home, Paco, quickly, before Olivia gets up."

"No! I won't leave you."

"Don't worry. My family will find me soon. I need to rest now." And she put her head down and closed her eyes.

Paco didn't leave. He sat right next to Coco and threw his head back. He took a deep breath, he opened his mouth wide, and bringing the sound up from deep in his chest as Professor Pewmount had taught him, he began to howl.

Paco howled louder than he had ever howled before.

He howled deeper than he had ever howled before. He howled like a big dog would howl. He howled with all the strength in his Chihuahua's body because he needed to wake Coco's family right then.

And he did.

He heard Sandy's voice drift through an open window. "Dad! Dad! What's that noise? It sounds like a dog in trouble."

He heard Sandy's father call out, "Something's wrong out there. That dog's howling for a reason."

Paco heard two sets of footsteps running through the house and pounding across wooden floors. But he didn't move. He kept howling until he saw the back door open. He kept howling until the second he heard Sandy's father yell, "Coco! It's Coco! Sandy, call the vet! Coco's hurt!" Only then did Paco, his heart a cold stone in his chest, his spirits lower than they had ever been in his whole life, run out of the yard, across the street, down the red bricks of the narrow alley, and race lickety-split for home.

No one stirred inside Paco's house when he squirmed through the doggy door. Olivia and her mother were still asleep. Quietness softly filled the rooms. Paco let out a deep sigh. He was so happy to be back.

He trotted over to his favorite spot on the recliner. He hopped up and burrowed under the afghan that

Grammie had knitted. All he wanted to do was go to sleep.

His nose hit something hard. His head jerked up. *What did Norma-Jean and Little Annie do this time!* he thought, getting mad and forgetting how tired he was. He pushed aside the afghan to see what was filling his seat.

A neat pile of doggy treats sat on the cushion of the recliner.

A little meow came from the top of the chair. Norma-Jean asked, "Are you all right? We were very worried."

"We thought you might be hungry," Little Annie said.

"*Gracias*, my sisters," Paco managed to say, his throat closing up with tears. The cats had waited up for him just like they'd said they would. They really did like him. They really were his *family.*

Putting his chin down on the doggy treats, Paco stopped acting brave. And only then did he begin to cry.

CHAPTER 7

There was a robber here last night! A robber with a big knife!" Sandy said. His eyes widened with excitement, and he used his hands to show how huge the knife must have been. "Coco fought him off. That's how she got cut so bad."

The sunshine bright in her eyes, Olivia, Paco's precious little girl, sat on the back steps of Sandy's house and listened to her friend. "A robber? How do you know? Did you see him?"

"No, Dad and I didn't see anybody. Coco had already chased him away. But it must have been a robber."

"Why? Was anything stolen?"

"Yeah! Coco's backpack was gone. And the refrigerator door was wide open. Dad checked and he said two bottles of water were missing and—and—and a whole pack of hot dogs! I think the robber put them in the backpack. He would have taken other stuff too, I bet. But Coco got him!"

Paco, who was lying at Olivia's feet, put his paws over his eyes and moaned.

The girl looked at the little dog. "I don't think Paco's feeling well."

"He looks OK to me."

"I don't know. He's just not himself." Olivia shook her head so that her brown curls danced up and down. "I can't put my finger on it. I dragged him out of the house today. He always runs for the door when I say we're going for a car ride. He loves coming over here. But this time he didn't want to move. He kept whimpering and wouldn't get out of the recliner."

As if on cue, Paco whimpered again. His whole body ached like a bad tooth. Tears welled up in his eyes. He squeezed them shut to keep from crying.

"See, like that! Maybe he's in pain."

The only pain Paco felt was all inside his heart. The phone had rung early that morning. When he had heard Olivia say, "Hello? Sandy?" his chest had gotten tight. He couldn't breathe. He had felt so afraid that Sandy brought bad news about Coco. When he had heard Livy say, "So she's going to be OK?" his breath came out in a whoosh. So did more tears.

He also heard Livy say she would come over that afternoon and bring Paco along.

Paco didn't want to go. He didn't want to face Coco. He stubbornly refused to leave the recliner, even though Livy dressed him in the new denim jacket she had bought at the mall. A picture of a Chihuahua riding a motorcycle adorned the coat's back, under the words "Hot Dog!"

He looked good, but that didn't lift his spirits at all.

Now Paco moped on the concrete path behind Sandy's house. Guilt settled on him like a black cloud. Coco had gotten hurt because of him, no matter what she said. He whimpered again, but this time no one noticed because all they could hear was a wild frenzy of yips and excited barking.

"Tommy and B-Boy are here!" Sandy yelled. "Wait until I tell Tommy about the robber."

"Hi, Tommy!" Olivia's face lit up as if someone had turned a spotlight on her.

The red-haired boy jumped off his bike. He dug into his jacket pocket and pulled out a pack of gummy worms. "Open your mouth and I'll give you one," he told Olivia.

Olivia giggled. She put her head back and opened her mouth like a baby bird. Tommy dropped in a big, fat, orange gummy worm.

"Hey! I want one too."

"Sure, Sandy. Here, catch!" Tommy flipped a yellow worm over to his friend. Then he popped a green one in his own mouth. They all chewed while Sandy told him about the robber that Coco had driven away, risking her own life, and getting a deep cut on her paw.

"She lost a lot of blood," Sandy explained. "She has to take it easy for a whole week. She has to wear this big stupid collar that looks like a funnel so she can't bite at the stitches. But she won't limp or anything once it heals. That's what the vet said."

"That's great," Tommy said.

"But you know what?" Sandy asked.

"What?" Olivia and Tommy said together.

"Dad and I never heard Coco barking. We heard another dog howling. That's what woke us up. It wasn't Coco. It's a mystery, that's what Dad says, anyway."

"How weird," Olivia said, as Tommy stretched out another gummy worm in her direction but kept it dangling right out of her reach.

"Stop being a tease, Tommy," she laughed, not sounding a bit mad.

"Yeah, it's strange, and what's even stranger…" Sandy hesitated.

"What?" Olivia and Tommy again said at the same time.

"I thought at first it was—no, it couldn't be, but I thought for a minute—"

"What!" the two other children yelled.

"I thought the other dog sounded just like Paco. But that's impossible."

"Paco?" Olivia said. "Paco was asleep on the recliner all night. It couldn't have been him."

"I know. It seemed crazy to me too. But still—some dog *was* howling and woke us up. The vet said that saved Coco's life. We got her to the vet just in time."

"No! Was it that bad?" Olivia shivered all of a sudden.

Sandy nodded, his face solemn.

Paco whimpered again, his head hanging down.

"Howling. Here. Last night," B-Boy put his mouth close to Paco's ear and whispered. "It *was* you, was it?"

Paco nodded. "*Sí*, it was all my fault."

"You cut Coco?"

"Of course I didn't cut Coco," Paco snapped. B-Boy was the most annoying Jack Russell terrier in the whole world.

"So what happened?" Suddenly B-Boy couldn't stay still another second. He began running up and down the steps, up and down the steps, making Paco dizzy just watching him.

"If you must know, we went looking for the werewolf, but the werewolf found us first. He chased us. We ran through a junkyard, and Coco cut her foot."

"You're joking!" B-Boy skidded to a stop. His eyes turned into saucers. "You've got to be kidding, right?"

"*Ay, caramba!* Do I sound like I'm kidding! I nearly got my best friend killed. All because I took your stupid advice." Paco stood up, his tail stiff. Maybe he'd feel better if he got in a fight with B-Boy.

"Don't blame me!" B-Boy barked.

"I will too blame you!" Paco barked back.

B-Boy rushed behind Paco, darted in, and nipped the tip of Paco's tail.

Paco whirled around and growled in B-Boy's direction, showing his small white teeth.

"Half-pint! You can't get me!" B-Boy barked.

Enraged, Paco leaped at B-Boy and tried to bite his leg.

"Hey! Stop!" Tommy yelled. Paco backed away from B-Boy, but he kept growling. He was so mad.

"Livy, what's wrong with Paco?"

"Paco! What are you doing? What's wrong with you!" Olivia's voice scolded. She scooped up the little dog into her arms. "I told you he wasn't himself. Maybe I should take him home."

"No, don't go! I think B-Boy started it. He jumped on Paco or something," Sandy said. "They'll be okay. Let's go in and see Coco. I know she must feel left out if she heard our voices out here."

Leaving the backyard and the bright sunshine of the afternoon, they all went inside.

"Don't you dare laugh at me." Coco lay in her dog bed, her brown head at the bottom of what looked like a huge white funnel that circled her neck. Curtains covered the windows, making the room dim. Darkness lingered in the corners.

"Hey, hey, Coco." B-Boy ran over and sniffed her up and down. "Nice collar. You look like a flower. A daisy."

Paco stayed back, his head drooping. "I'm so sorry, Coco," he sniffed.

"Come over here, Paco." Coco's voice was soft. She looked terribly weary, and her nose was pale.

Paco slowly walked closer. He couldn't meet her eyes.

"Look at me."

He raised his head.

"See. I'm OK. You saved my life. I'm going to be fine."

Paco looked down again, blinking away tears. "I feel terrible," he whimpered.

"Listen to me, Paco!" Coco's voice sounded stronger than she looked. "We had a great adventure. And you know what? My family calls me their hero. They think I fought off a robber with a knife! I didn't get in a bit of trouble for taking the hot dogs or losing my backpack. Instead, I'm being pampered. Sandy even made me this medal."

She lifted her head so Paco could see a blue ribbon with a silver foil medal hanging around her neck underneath the big white funnel. Written on the medal were the words *World's Greatest Dog.*

Coco's voice turned gentle. "See, everything turned out great."

Paco looked up, light coming back into his eyes. "It did? You're not mad at me?"

"I'm not mad at you. Not even a little bit. Come on over here. You look worn out. I'm a little tired. Let's take a nap."

Paco squeezed into Coco's dog bed. He curled up next to her. He closed his eyes and smiled. He felt comforted by her presence. All was right in his world.

"Hey hey Coco! What about me?" B-Boy was running around the dog bed, first circling in one direction, then stopping and running back.

"You can climb in too," Coco said.

B-Boy grinned. He jumped into the dog bed and pushed his way into a spot next to Paco. He plopped down and fidgeted, trying to get comfortable.

Paco frowned. *Nothing is ever perfect,* he thought and wriggled away from B-Boy. Then, feeling happier, he fell into a deep sleep and didn't dream.

But Coco didn't dare to sleep. She kept a close watch over her two little friends. Even though she had told Paco that everything had turned out great, it really hadn't. She knew the werewolf had followed them to town the night before, and she didn't know why. Or what he planned to do.

CHAPTER 8

All afternoon the children sat around the kitchen table playing Uno. They tried to be very quiet so they didn't disturb Coco. They popped popcorn in the microwave. They made nachos. The hours passed. Paco and B-Boy slept. Coco pretended to doze.

Then the sound of a persistent doorbell broke the quiet.

Sandy threw down his cards. "It's Victoria! She's supposed to come over."

The noise jarred B-Boy awake. He barked wildly. "The door! The bell! The door! The bell! Get them!" He jumped out of bed and dashed toward the front hall.

Paco lifted his head from his cozy spot in Coco's doggy bed. He raised an eyebrow. *Victoria? Maybe Natasha is here too,* he thought.

Much to his surprise, his heart didn't race. He didn't feel an ounce of excitement about seeing the sleek, elegant Afghan hound again. He still thought she was beautiful, but he didn't want to be her boyfriend anymore.

Why bother getting up to see her? Paco heaved a huge sigh. He wasn't ever going to turn into a werewolf now, and Natasha would never love a tiny Chihuahua. *No importa. I don't want to be a big bad werewolf after all. I don't want anything to do with werewolves, muchas gracias!* He shook his head sadly, and his dog tags jingled. He decided he might as well go back to sleep.

But out in the hall, something was happening that changed Paco's mind.

A wave of unhappiness washed over Olivia when the doorbell rang, and Sandy announced that it was Victoria. She enjoyed playing cards with the boys. Although Olivia liked Victoria, things changed when she joined the group. The two boys acted dumb to get Victoria's attention. They seemed to forget Olivia existed.

It just wasn't as much fun when Victoria was there.

So when Sandy went to answer the door, Olivia decided to get Paco and go home. It was nearly dinnertime anyway.

Then she heard Sandy ask, "What's the matter?" and the sound of Victoria crying. Forgetting she wanted to leave, Olivia ran toward the front door. Tommy trotted along right behind her.

Back in the dimly lit bedroom, Paco's ears perked up at the sounds of crying and running feet.

Coco let out an anguished yip. "Something's very

wrong!" she cried. Right away, her thoughts focused on the werewolf. *He did something terrible.* She just knew it!

Coco tried to stand, but she couldn't and sat back down. "Find out what's going on, Paco, please."

Paco scampered into the hall just in time to hear Victoria wail, "Natasha is missing!"

Paco's heart lurched. *Natasha? Missing?*

All the children started talking at once. "What happened? What do you mean?"

"She's gone," Victoria gulped back her sobs. "We can't find her. My brother Michael took her along this morning when he ran in the park. He always does. He said that all of a sudden, Natasha became very excited. She started barking as if she saw something. The fur on her back stood up. She growled and looked toward some trees. Michael thought he saw the shape of something big.

"He went to grab her collar and she took off. She raced into the woods. Michael heard terrible barking and growling. He followed her. But when he got to the woods, she was gone.

"And she never came back." Victoria began sobbing again.

"Did you look for her?" Tommy asked.

Victoria nodded. "Mumsy, Poppy, and I rode around in the car. We asked everybody!"

"Did anyone see her?" Olivia tried to keep her voice calm. She didn't want to sound upset, but she felt very shaken. She saw the streaks of tears on Victoria's rosy cheeks. The pretty girl's nose turned red as a cherry and started to run. Olivia handed her a tissue, then put a comforting arm around Victoria's shoulders.

Victoria blew her nose and said, "We went to the police station. An officer said somebody in a corner house on Edgemount Street had reported two dogs running loose and heading for the interstate. One of them sounded like Natasha, but the other one—the other one was, he was—"

"What?" Tommy asked at the same time Sandy did.

Victoria shrugged. "Uh, not really a dog. The policeman said it might have been a wolf, or a coyote. He called animal control. He thought the big animal could be dangerous."

Paco froze. He looked at B-Boy. B-Boy looked at Paco.

"It's the werewolf," Paco whispered. "He must have followed us into town."

"Noooo!" B-Boy's brown button eyes looked wild.

Paco nodded. "I think so, yes."

"Then what happened?" Olivia asked Victoria.

"The policeman told us to go home. He'll call us if they find Natasha. Animal control promised to send a team with a capture van out tomorrow. Poppy said we shouldn't search anymore, to let animal control do it. But I'm so scared—maybe the big animal will hurt her by then. Maybe she'll never come back!"

"That's true! We can't wait. She might run too far.

Or she might get hurt. We have to look for her *tonight*," Tommy decided.

"We do?" Olivia's voice sounded shaky.

"Right!" yelled Sandy. "We can ride our bikes and cover a lot of ground."

"Great idea!" Tommy high-fived him.

"But I don't have my bike here," Olivia protested.

"Neither do I," sniffed Victoria who had stopped crying.

"We'll have to meet up later, that's all. But—"

"But what?" Olivia said.

"We better not tell our parents." Tommy's face looked sly.

"Nope. They'd never let us go," Sandy agreed.

B-Boy was leaping up and down, barking wildly. He didn't like this. "Paco, do something! Stop them!" he cried.

Paco thought fast. He raced to the doggy door and ran to Tommy's bike. He took a deep breath and attacked the front tire, biting it as hard as he could with his little white teeth. He heard a hiss of air.

Then he rushed back in. The children were sitting around the kitchen table, talking, making plans about how they were going to get together with their bikes and sneak off to look for Natasha.

Paco motioned to B-Boy to follow him into the darkened room where Coco lay. He needed to tell his best friend that they had a *problema*. A *gran problema*.

"The werewolf followed us!" Coco cried. "We led him right to Natasha's house. He must have lurked there until she went to the park. She's so pretty. He dognapped her."

Paco snorted. "Maybe he did. But maybe she ran off with him. She likes big, dangerous dogs. She said so herself."

"Paco!" Coco scolded. "I don't believe she ran away with him. I believe she was trying to protect Victoria's brother. The werewolf overpowered her and carried her off. Otherwise she would have come back."

"That's bad. That's terrible." B-Boy yelped.

"It is." Worry lines appeared on Coco's forehead. "Worse, the children are going to look for her." Her soft brown eyes looked right into Paco's. "Do you understand what I'm saying, Paco?"

"*Sí?*" He didn't know what Coco was getting at.

Her eyes bore into his. "We must keep the children safe. We can't let the werewolf get *them*. That's more important than anything else."

"*Ay! Claro!*" Paco agreed

"But *I* can't walk." Coco's frown lines deepened. "It's up to you and B-Boy to stop them from going to look for Natasha."

"Me? And B-Boy?" Paco lay down by Coco's doggy bed. His misery blanketed him with woe. "I don't know how. I don't know what to do."

"You bit Tommy's tire. You did. It was smart to do that," B-Boy offered, then stared intently at his tail. He considered chasing it. When he felt especially nervous, he did stuff like that.

Paco shook his head from side to side. "No. It was dumb to bite the tire. He'll just fix it. I don't know how we can keep them from looking for Natasha."

"And if they look for Natasha they'll find—" B-Boy didn't finish his thought. Instead, he needed to chase his tail. He started whirling in a circle.

"B-Boy!" Paco yipped. "*Alto!* Stop it! We have to think."

"Can't think. Can't think. Must run." B-Boy twirled around and around.

Paco turned to Coco. "B-Boy's not so good at thinking. What should we do?"

Coco closed her eyes. Then she opened them. "We're looking at this the wrong way. I have an idea. We *can't* stop them."

Paco smacked his forehead with his paw. "*Ay! Ay! Ay!* I know that. That's not much of an idea, Coco."

"But think about what we *can* do. We know where

the werewolf lives. So we know where Natasha is. The children don't know that, not yet, anyway. If you and B-Boy find Natasha first and bring her back, the children won't have any reason to look for her."

B-Boy stopped whirling and looked at Coco, his eyes filled with admiration. "That's brilliant!"

"Wait a minute, wait a minute," Paco sputtered. "B-Boy and I are *little* dogs. The werewolf is huge and mean and dangerous. And what if—"

"What?" Coco asked.

"What if Natasha likes him—" Paco could barely stand to say what he was thinking. His voice became so soft the rest of his words faded away to a whisper, "and she doesn't want to come back."

"Paco!" Coco cried, angry at first. Then she repeated his name with kindness. "Paco, that's not going to happen."

Coco understood her Mexican friend better than he did himself. She knew his feelings were hurt. "Natasha loves Victoria with a dog's loyal heart. She would fight to the death to protect her or her brother. She would never willingly leave her family. Yes, she likes to run free and far and fast. She's a hound, you know. The desire is in her. But not this time. She'd come back if she could. But I *know* she can't. The werewolf followed her to the park and dognapped her."

"Awful. Terrible. Poor Natasha," B-Boy ran in circles around the doggy bed.

"Yes, it is terrible," Coco nodded. "Paco, you and B-Boy have to rescue Natasha before the children reach Mount Diablo. We can't let them run into the werewolf."

Paco knew she was right, and yet he feared he couldn't do it. "I'm *muy poco,* too small and weak to bring her home—even with B-Boy helping. What if the werewolf sees us and stops us? What if we have to fight him?"

Coco mentally counted to ten. It wouldn't do to yell. She couldn't go with them, so she must help Paco find the courage to do what must be done without her. When she spoke, her voice was calm. She hid her frustration well. "Paco, my dearest friend, you might not be *big,* but you are *smart.* Think! Who else can go with you? Who else would help you fight the werewolf if you have to? You're only weak if you go alone. Do you understand?"

Paco stared at her. Suddenly, his thoughts lit up like the dark earth when the sun rises in the morning. "*Sí!* I do! I'll ask the wild ones to help us." Then his mind dimmed a little. "Do you think there's time to ask them?"

"Yes, I do! The children won't sneak away until after supper. Tommy will have to fix his flat tire. You will have a good head start on them."

"*Sí! Muy bien!*" He looked at B-Boy.

B-Boy grinned. "*Muy bien* right back at you, Paco! You're right!" He ran over and gave Paco a high five.

Coco's sharp voice got their attention. "You'll have

a head start, but the children will be on bikes. They can ride faster than you can run. You'll have to use some tricks to slow them down. Even then, it's going to be very hard. Paco, you have to use your brains. You have to *think*!"

"*Bueno!* I will!" Determination strengthened the little dog's backbone. He stood up as tall as he could. Although a cruel white worm of doubt was wiggling around in his stomach, he wouldn't let Coco or B-Boy know that. And he would never let the werewolf hurt Olivia. He took that one thought in his teeth and bit hard. He'd hang onto it. No doubts or fears would stop him.

CHAPTER 9

Paco slipped out the doggy door and into his back-yard as soon as he and Olivia returned home. The smell of food cooking in the kitchen followed him into the evening air. The family would be eating soon. Afterward Olivia would make up an excuse to go back to Sandy's and meet the others.

Paco didn't overhear all the details of the children's scheme, but he knew that much. He shivered with nerves and worry, his little body trembling from the tip of his nose to the end of his tail.

He hurried. He trotted down the walk until he got to the dirt path through the weeds. He knew that Pewy, the old skunk, slept through the daytime hours somewhere near the tumbled-down-stone wall, but his den was well hidden. Paco had never found it.

The Chihuahua stood up on his hind legs and stretched himself as tall as he could so his voice would carry. He called out, "Pewy! Can you hear me! Professor Pewmount, wake up. I need help."

No one answered. The weeds didn't stir.

Paco called again. He listened. He heard nothing. He called again, now getting very worried that the skunk wouldn't wake up until it was too late.

fee - be
fee -

Suddenly he heard a chickadee began to sing loudly *dee dee dee*. It came again. *Dee dee dee dee*. Paco's ears stood up. Then the bird gave a two-note whistle, *fee beee, fee beee*.

Was the bird talking to him? Paco yipped, "I need help! I need help!"

Dee dee dee went the chickadee. Then louder, *DEE DEE DEE.*

Then, riding gently on the breeze, a sleepy voice said, "I'm coming, I'm coming. Keep your shirt on." The weeds shook. A black and white tail waved above them. Finally, the fat skunk poked his pointed nose into the open.

"That you, Paco?"

"It's me! I was looking for you." Joy flooded the Chihuahua at the sight of his old friend.

"Guess you were. That noisy bird woke me up. Said you needed help." The skunk waddled onto the lawn and sat down with a plop. "Let me catch my breath. Smart of you to tell a chickadee. They're the biggest gossips in the forest. They can't keep their mouths shut. They always know everything," he grumped.

Paco decided that was a good thing to remember.

"So what's wrong, my little *amigo?*" Pewmount asked.

Paco, talking so fast he barely took a breath, told him the whole story.

Pewmount didn't interrupt. He listened without taking his licorice eyes from Paco's worried face. When the tiny dog finished, the skunk asked, "What exactly do you want the forest creatures to do? They're good soldiers, but not good generals, you understand?"

Paco had given that very question a lot of thought since Coco told him he had to *think*. He was good at plans, he really was.

Paco took a deep breath, exhaled, and said, "*Sí*. I need three things done. First, I need the wild ones to play some tricks that will slow the children down. That will give me and B-Boy time to get to the junkyard and find Natasha."

"Mmmmmm. You have any ideas who should play the tricks?"

"I think so." And Paco told him.

Pewmount considered Paco's suggestions. He decided they might work, with a little luck. "OK, what's the second thing you need done?" he asked, and his eyes got very worried when Paco told him. "It's dangerous," he said.

"*Sí*," Paco agreed.

"But you're right. It must be done. Now, what is the third thing?"

"I need a very fast and cunning animal to lure the

werewolf away from Natasha, so B-Boy and I can reach her and tell her she has to come home."

"Fast and cunning?" Pewmount mused.

Just then, Paco felt a poke. He turned around. Norma-Jean sat there. So did Little Annie.

"We heard everything," the gray cat said.

"We want to help," the black cat added.

Together they said, "We're fast and cunning!" and they gave each other a shoulder bump.

"You're only cats!" Paco protested.

"Exactly!" Norma-Jean grinned.

"That's the point," Little Annie laughed. "Any dog will chase a cat!"

"Even a dog who might be a werewolf!" Norma-Jean chimed in.

Paco's heart sank to his toes. "No! I can't let you. He might catch you. You might get hurt."

Norma-Jean rolled her eyes. "Did *you* ever catch us?"

"Well, no."

"We intend to go anyway." Little Annie put her paws on her hips and cocked her head to one side. "Whether you want us to or not! Olivia belongs to us too! We have to protect her."

"I—I—don't know what to say."

Professor Pewmount cleared his throat. "You don't need to say anything. If any animals can fool this great beast, they can. Those two are the sneakiest, most mischievous cats I ever met."

Norma-Jean and Little Annie grinned. "He's right! We are!" They said together.

Pewmount spoke up again. "Now, Mr. Paco, my *muy poco amigo,* my small friend, as my sainted mother used to say, *There's a time to talk and a time to do.* I better get *doing* if we are to slow those children down."

With those final words, he turned around and disappeared back into the weeds.

To Paco, the minutes passed by as if they were in a race with each other. The sun dropped like a stone toward the horizon. Long evening shadows stretched across the lawn with the swiftness of spilled water.

Paco made a quick decision. "Let's leave right now!" he cried out to Norma-Jean and Little Annie.

They didn't wait until the family finished dinner. They didn't worry whether or not they'd be missed. As if a starting gun had fired, Paco and his cats took off running. They bounded over the tumbled-down-stone wall. They raced along the narrow alley, and they crossed three streets—being careful to look both ways first. They dove under the hedges at Tommy Thompson's house. Paco gave a prearranged signal: *yip, yippity yip yip, bark bark!*

Seconds later, B-Boy climbed out of a window and raced across the lawn.

"Go, go, go!" the Jack Russell barked as he scampered

past them and down the sidewalk. "Tommy's getting ready to leave."

The facts are the facts. The truth cannot be ignored. Short legs do not run very fast or get very far.

The four friends raced away from Tommy Thompson's house, paws a blur of motion, tails straight as rudders. But after they ran and ran, and ran and ran, and still didn't reach the white highway, Paco called for a halt.

He needed to catch his breath. He puffed. He huffed. He remembered that it had taken hours for Coco and him to reach Mount Diablo.

He turned an anguished face toward the other animals. "This won't work. We're *muy lento,* too slow."

B-Boy, Norma-Jean, and Little Annie agreed.

"But we can't give up," B-Boy insisted.

"We won't give up!" The two cats put in their two cents.

"We're not!" Paco barked. "We need another plan. Let me think for a minute."

Paco squeezed his eyes closed. Then he opened them and stared at the sky. The clear blue of an early summer evening did not reflect the dark worry in his mind. He really did not know what to do.

But he did not give up. He kept looking upward but seeing inward. He stayed still. He thought hard. Then his ears quivered, detecting the muted rumble of semi-trucks traveling the white highway in the distance. And, then, Paco got another great idea.

At the highway rest area, row after row of huge tractor trailers filled the parking spaces. Eighteen-wheelers, belching black smoke, pulled in off the highway, while others, their engines thundering, pulled back onto the interstate.

The noise frightened the four small animals, but it didn't stop them from coming closer. They slunk around the edge of asphalt, staying on the grass. They crouched low and stayed out of sight. All the while, their eyes scanned the windows of the idling big rigs looking for what Paco had described to them.

"There!" B-Boy yipped. "Over there. In the green one. Do you see him?"

"I sure hear him." Little Annie put her paws over her ears.

Not twenty feet away, the black head of a fox-like dog called a Schipperke suddenly poked out of the open passenger-side window of a tall truck cab. The dog's front feet did a little dance on the window ledge as it barked loudly and joyously. "Hey! Hey! Who are you? Hey! Hey! Come on over! Hey! It's OK. I like cats. Hey! Come say hello!"

"Let's go!" Paco yelled and made a dash for the green cab. His friends followed. Standing in the parking lot, they introduced themselves to the dog high above them in the cab window.

The black dog was called Teddy. He was glad to meet them. But, he asked, what were they doing here at a truck rest stop?

Talking quickly, Paco told their story. He ended by saying they needed a ride to Mount Diablo to save their children. "So you are going that way? *Sí*? Is the driver coming back soon? We're running out of time."

"Don't worry. Don't worry," the black dog barked. "Driver Jim only went to the restroom. He's coming right back. We're on our way home. Don't worry. I'll help."

"Thank you!" the posse below yelled.

Teddy the Schipperke grinned a doggy smile. "Tell you what. I'll get this door open. You hop in. Hide behind the seat. Jim won't even notice. When we get to Mount Diablo, I'll tell him I need to 'go.' You know what I mean. Soon as he opens the door, you guys run."

"You sure?" Paco thought about all the things that could go wrong—in particular, what if driver Jim didn't stop when Teddy asked to "go"?

"Absolute-ally! Come on. Hurry. I see Jim starting this way."

Teddy pressed down on the door handle. He pushed the cab door open wide enough for the cats to clamber up. Then B-Boy, whose legs worked like coiled springs, bounced into the cab without a bit of trouble.

Tiny Paco jumped only as far as the running board. "I can't make it," he whimpered.

"Hang on!" B-Boy leaped back out. He got behind Paco and pushed. Teddy reached down and grabbed Paco's collar with his teeth. With a heave and a ho, Paco found himself inside the truck. B-Boy came in right behind him just as a tall man wearing bib overalls and a red-and-black plaid jacket shouted, "Hey! The truck door's open! Teddy! Stay!"

His face turning white, his heavy boots going thud on the pavement, Jim the truck driver rushed to his vehicle and slammed the cab door shut. It narrowly missed Paco's tail.

Jim peered up at Teddy, whose head poked over the window ledge again. "How the heck did you get that door open? Gee whiz, little guy, that was close." Jim took off his cap and scratched his head. He studied the door. Not seeing anything amiss, he went around the truck to get in on the driver's side, muttering, "Doggone it. Near took ten years off my life, seeing that door open. Could have lost my dog. Doggone it!"

Jim turned on the engine. He changed the gears. He

pressed the gas, and the eighteen-wheeler rolled back onto the highway. He flipped on the radio and sang along with a country song. Jim sang loudly and not very well, but he sang with gusto.

Squatting down behind the passenger seat, the little animals listened to Jim bellow out some words about being on the road again. They huddled together. They could feel each other's hearts beating. But they only heard Jim sing three more tunes before Teddy started whining and scratching at the window.

The long journey along the white highway took Coco and Paco many hours to travel. Now it took just a few minutes.

Jim looked over at the black dog. "You got to go already?"

Whine, whine cried Teddy. He circled around several times on the seat just to make his point that the situation was urgent.

"Hang on, hang on, I'll pull over at this exit," Jim promised, his voice kind. He did love his dog a great deal and didn't mind.

He eased the truck onto the off-ramp. Paco spotted the overhead exit sign through the truck window. It was for Mount Diablo. Teddy got it exactly right. He heaved a sigh of relief.

As soon as Jim opened the door on Teddy's side of the truck, two cats and two dogs jumped out and scattered as fast as they could.

"Holy Hannah!" Jim gasped, his eyes as big as dinner plates. "Where did they come from?"

Teddy barked loudly.

Jim began to laugh. "So you picked me up some hitchhikers, did you?" Then the truck driver smiled so wide it made his cheeks ache. Whistling another song from the radio, he snapped on Teddy's leash and lifted him down from the cab. Jim looked forward to telling his wife about what Teddy had done *this* time.

Meanwhile, B-Boy, Norma-Jean, and Little Annie scampered along behind Paco until they reached a fork in the road. Without hesitation, the Chihuahua took the white way to the right. "It's not much longer," Paco called out.

"I wonder where the children are?" B-Boy asked.

"I wonder too." Paco felt a squeeze of anxiety in his chest, but he didn't slow down. He had to have faith in Pewmount and the plan. He ran on.

CHAPTER 10

S uccess owes much to luck. It owes more to good planning. Most of the time it needs a good dose of both.

Professor Pewmount's sainted mother told him that.

The wise old skunk got busy after talking with Paco. He called a meeting with the nosy chickadee who woke him, two red squirrels who were eavesdropping in a nearby tree, and five loud-mouthed blue jays he happened to know personally. He asked them to take Paco's request for help to the wild creatures.

The Professor was much respected by everyone, a true senator of the forest. He got a quick response. Birds, insects, and four-legged forest animals of all kinds showed up at his den. He didn't have to twist any arms to make some of them agree to play tricks on the children. Animals loved to outwit humans, and Paco's ideas were grand. Also, all wild creatures felt strongly about protecting their young.

And then Pewmount turned to some of the others. He chose them because they were the swiftest— they must travel a long way in a very short time—and because they had some very special talents. He explained Paco's second request. They listened. They asked a few questions. They agreed to do it, even though it sounded very dangerous. They understood that this terrible creature must be driven away or destroyed before it ate them all, one by one.

"You must hurry," Pewy said to these bravest of the brave. "If you are late, it will be too late…for all of us."

They left as fast as they could.

Then Pewy turned to those whose job was to delay the children. "Chickadee will be your spotter. She'll fly above the children. Listen for her signal. Then move in!"

"Why is Coco howling?" Olivia asked Sandy. She stood next to her bike in Sandy's backyard where the four children gathered.

"She didn't want me to go out. Each time I walked away, she struggled to get up and started crying. I hated to leave her. How long do you think we'll be gone, Tommy?"

"Let's see." Tommy looked at his wristwatch. "It's nearly six now. We've got two good hours and maybe even three before dark. We can cover a lot of ground by then."

"Where are we going?" Olivia's face looked worried.

"We need to start where Natasha was last spotted with the big animal. Victoria, do you know that exact place?"

"Yes, I'll take you to the street. It's not far from here."

"Great. They were headed toward the highway. We'll follow the same route." Tommy threw his leg over the bar of his bike and prepared to push off.

Olivia didn't move. "Wait a minute. What happens when we get to the highway? We can't ride our bikes along the interstate."

Tommy grinned. "I already thought of that. I Googled a map on my computer. A hiking trail runs in the same direction as the highway, but through the woods. It leads toward Mount Diablo. We can ride there. OK?"

"That sounds OK, but—" Olivia's voice held a heavy load of doubt. "Let's watch the time. I wouldn't want to be in the woods when it's getting dark."

"Me neither," Sandy spoke up.

"Ahhh, don't be sissies. Nothing out there can hurt us. Our bikes have headlights if it gets too dark to see. I even brought a megaphone for Victoria to call Natasha."

Victoria looked at Tommy as if he was her hero. "Oh, Tommy, you're always so smart." Victoria smiled, showing perfect pearly teeth.

A red blush crept up Tommy's neck and spread roses into his freckled cheeks. "I brought a leash and some dog treats too." He gave her a dreamy look for just a second before his voice filled with command. "Get on your bikes, gang! We'd better get going."

Olivia still didn't move. She heard something, and it wasn't Tommy. "Shhhhh. Wait a minute. Listen. What's that sound?"

"That's just a chickadee," Tommy dismissed her. "It's nothing! Come on!"

"No, not the *dee dee dee*. Listen again. Is it a cat? Not quite like a cat, but something crying—oh, look up!"

The children lifted their faces toward the sky.

A big gray gull flew over the housetops and circled above them. He was calling in a high-pitched mewing voice. Another gray gull quickly appeared, calling back. Then two more. Then a squadron of ten. Soon, the sky turned dark with the gulls. Their cries filled the air.

"I never saw this many gulls above my backyard before." Sandy's voice held a hint of wonder.

"I once saw this many at the seashore," Victoria remembered. "A little boy tossed cheese doodles in the air. Dozens of gulls came out of nowhere and started fighting for the food. And all of a sudden—"

Before she could finish, a large gull folded back its wings and dove low over the children. Something went splat on the payment. Another gull swooped down toward Tommy. A white blob hit the fender of Tommy's bike.

"Hey! Quit that!" he yelled. A third gull flew directly above his head. Something wet smacked down on his hair.

Then blobs of white started dropping from the sky like a hailstorm.

One hit Sandy's shirt. He stared at it. Understanding hit him like the flash from a camera. "It's bird poop! They're pooping on us! Run! Run for the garage!"

"My hair!" Victoria screamed. She dropped her ten-speed and raced toward the garage door. White blobs streaked her long golden tresses.

"Euccch. I've got bird poop on my arm!" Olivia cried. She pushed her bike as fast as she could toward shelter while poop rained onto the ground, turning it white.

The seagull poop attack lasted only a minute or two, but the damage was done.

As soon as the gulls flew away, Sandy hurried into the house for wipes and paper towels. He handed them out. The children cleaned themselves and their bikes.

The minutes ticked by.

Victoria held back tears as Olivia wiped the white stuff out of her hair. "Can you get it all?" she whimpered. "It's so gross."

"Don't worry. It's coming out. But you know, that was very weird," Olivia said when she finished helping Victoria. She cleaned her bare arms where the poop had landed and wiped the blotches off her shorts. "They seemed to be aiming at us."

"It's a bad omen." Sandy sounded terribly serious. "We've already lost some time. Maybe I shouldn't go."

"You are such a wimp." Tommy's voice held disgust. "It was just a lot of bird poop. Nobody got hurt."

Victoria turned her violet eyes filled with pleading toward Sandy. "Please go with us. I'm so worried about Natasha. We won't be long."

"I know, but—I don't like sneaking away. I told my Dad I was going to Victoria's."

"So what?" Tommy responded. "The rest of us said we're taking a swim in your pool. Look, nobody will know we're gone. We'll be home safe and sound before dark—and maybe we'll have Natasha with us! I bet we do." Tommy sounded confident.

Sandy pushed aside his worries. "You're right. Victoria needs us. Let's get going."

Tommy mounted his bike. The other children got on theirs. They pedaled out of the yard and into the quiet, tree-lined street.

"It's this way," Victoria called out. She took the lead.

Nobody noticed the lone chickadee flying behind them all.

CHAPTER 11

ever give up. Never. Never. Never.

Trotting up the white road toward the junk-yard, B-Boy stayed at Paco's side. The cats scampered behind in fits and starts. The evening light weakened, but the sun had not yet set. The way was bright and easy, but oh so very long. They had short legs. There was nothing they could do about it.

Finally the dank, dark tunnel of trees appeared ahead. They were approaching dangerous ground.

"*Alto!*" Paco yelled. Everyone stopped. "Let's review the plan before we get closer."

"I know it." Little Annie raised her hand. "Once we find Natasha and the werewolf, Norma-Jean and I will go off and find a very tall tree. Then we come back and get close to the werewolf. We make sure he spots us. We make sure he chases us. Then we make sure we climb all the way up to the top of the tree. To be safe. We tease him from there. We keep him busy while you get Natasha and escape."

"And how will you know that Natasha is free?" Paco prompted.

"You'll give a signal—three short yips and one long bark. That's Morse code for V…V for victory." The cats and Paco watched shows about World War II on the History Channel quite a bit.

"*Sí! Claro!* You got it," Paco agreed. "Then what?"

"We stop teasing the werewolf. When he leaves, we get out of the tree. We run behind you down the white road and catch up to you at the highway," Norma-Jean added.

Paco frowned. *When he leaves…* He had thought the cats could keep the werewolf busy until he and B-Boy had safely rescued Natasha. But now something felt heavy in his belly, like a cannonball of doubt. What if the werewolf got suspicious and didn't stay by the tree? What if he spotted the dogs? What if he chased them— before the rest of Paco's plan could be put into place?

And what if Pewy didn't arrange the most important piece of the whole operation?

Paco gave himself a shake, and his dog tags jingled. He puffed out his chest. He straightened his tail. He must keep up morale. He must look like the commander-in-chief of this rescue mission.

He nodded. "*Sí. Claro.* That's it. We'd better get going." And they did.

They entered the tunnel of trees. The daylight

disappeared. Paco hadn't brought a flashlight. He had forgotten it. He was almost blind. He and B-Boy held on to the cats' tails as Norma-Jean and Little Annie, who could see very well in the dark, led the way.

They went deeper and deeper into the gloom. The nasty trash of the junkyard lurked along the edge of the road. Paco was back in the place of broken things. Then a glimmer of light appeared ahead. They saw the end of the tunnel.

Right before they returned into the light, where they could see but also be seen, Paco signaled that the group of four should stop.

He stood up on his hind legs and sniffed. He smelled something terrible, as terrible as the smell he and Coco had whiffed the other night. The creature— the *werewolf*—must be somewhere close. But Paco searched for another scent, one he knew very well: the sweet shampoo of Natasha's fresh-washed fur and the lovely odor of her doggy self.

His nose twitched. He inhaled deeply. The rank and rotten odor of the werewolf made him gasp, but underneath the ugliness lay a hint of something beautiful. With a tremble of excitement, he realized Natasha must be there.

"Straight ahead," he whispered.

The trees with their overhanging branches quickly thinned out. The dogs could again see in the weak evening sunlight reflected by the white road. Using their noses, they followed the awful smell down a narrow path that snaked through piles of broken household appliances, cement culverts big enough for a man to walk through, and smaller drainage pipes that lay like pick-up sticks in huge heaps.

When the smell—like rotten eggs and rotten cabbage and musty basements—became very strong, they knew the werewolf must be close. The four friends got down on their bellies. They crawled forward. Inch by inch, they moved forward until they got to the edge of a clearing. In the clearing, an old easy chair sat next to a potbellied stove. Next to that, a three-legged table held a huge pile of bones.

Paco and his friends froze where they were and didn't dare move. Fear raced through Paco's blood like a lightning strike. This was the lair of the werewolf, and the werewolf was right there in front of them! It sat on a three-legged stool in front of the three-legged table. It was munching, crunching, and wolfing down a bone.

Snap went the bone. *Slurp* went the werewolf.

Ay, ay, ay, went Paco.

The creature looked nothing like a real wolf. Wolves were handsome canines. The werewolf was loathsome. Dirty, tangled hair like curling gray wires covered it from head to toe—except where single coarse strands sprouted from the gigantic warts on its face. Long, brutal fangs glistened white in a huge, gaping mouth, and from these terrible teeth, spit dripped down in strings.

Cruel, beady eyes shone red in the firelight. And at the end of a nose as square and black as a lump of coal were nostrils as wide as the barrel of a shotgun.

Ugly the werewolf was, but it was also as big as a grizzly bear—and even scarier. Hard muscles rippled under its wiry coat. A big, curved knife hung from a belt around its protruding belly. And while the little animals watched, not daring to even breathe, it stood up and looked around. It grabbed a bone from the pile and used it as a toothpick to clean its cruel white teeth.

Then it paced to the far side of the clearing. It stood up on its two back legs. Its front legs hung down like a gorilla's long arms and ended in hairy knuckles that touched the ground. It growled a growl that made the ground shake. It hacked, coughed up a gob as big as a teacup, and spat it onto the ground. Then came a rumble from the werewolf's big belly, followed by the trumpet call of the loudest, longest, and stinkiest fart Paco had ever experienced.

This was not an ordinary animal.

This was a monster.

Ay, caramba! I wouldn't want to be anything like that! Paco thought. He was grateful he hadn't drunk rainwater out of a werewolf's footprint as the Internet had instructed him to.

Then he heard a whimper, and his heart nearly broke. Tied to a stake by a thick rope attached to her collar, Natasha lay at the far edge of the clearing. Her beautiful long coat hung down, matted and dull. Her eyes held a heartbreaking sorrow. She clearly did not want to stay here. Her whimper said she wanted to go home.

But how could he and B-Boy get her loose? Paco hadn't thought to bring a knife when he devised his wonderful plan. He suddenly realized that plans could be made, but they sometimes could not be made to work.

And time was running out. The children were on their way. They must be getting close by now. Paco needed to come up with an idea in a hurry. But the harder he tried to think, the less he thought of anything helpful.

Just then, one of the cats poked him on the shoulder. She used sign language to show him that the sisters were going off to look for a very tall tree—and then she pointed. The only trees in view were the ones that lined the white road.

Paco nodded, and the two felines scampered off.

Another problem with the plan! How could the dogs sneak back to the road if the werewolf were already on it? Paco shrugged. He didn't have a solution. Yet he couldn't let that stop him. They were so close to saving Natasha, they just had to succeed. Determination fueled his courage. He needed the heart of lion, not a dandelion.

His body trembling, his nerves tight, but his will strong, Paco hunkered down behind some pipes with B-Boy to wait for the cats to make their move.

And he looked around for the help he had requested from Professor Pewmount. He didn't see anything. He listened carefully. He didn't hear anything. He needed that help. And he needed it now.

Paco's nerves danced a jig inside his skin. His mouth became parched, his tongue dry. He was very thirsty. He had not only forgotten a flashlight and a knife, he had forgotten bottled water. He sniffed. He looked around. He noticed clear water dripping into a puddle from one of the pipes right behind them. He crawled over and began to lap it up. It was cool and wet on his tongue.

"Paco! Stop!" B-Boy whispered as loudly as he dared.

Paco picked up his head and whispered back. "Why? It's just rainwater. It's a little rusty, but it tastes fine."

"No, not that. Look!" B-Boy pointed. "Look at the puddle."

Paco did. He stared for minute, until he realized he wasn't drinking out of a puddle at all. The water was pooled in a footprint—a dog-like footprint, but much bigger than a dog's paw.

"You're drinking from the werewolf's footprint!" B-Boy hissed.

Paco's eyes got very wide. His heart thudded. "Oh no! What have I done?" he gasped. "What have I done?"

CHAPTER 12

Meanwhile, in town, an elderly woman was sweeping her front walk. She had almost finished when she noticed four children riding bikes down the street. She stared at them. They lifted their heads and stared at her too. One raised a hand to wave.

The old woman hoped they weren't out to make trouble. She gripped her broom tighter.

They came closer and closer. They stopped at her gate and got off their bicycles.

She peered through her spectacles at them. They didn't look like bad children, except maybe the red-haired boy with a face covered with freckles. He might not be bad, but he carried mischief in his eyes. She meant Tommy Thompson, and of course she was right.

"Hello," Tommy called out through a megaphone, which made his voice very loud.

The old woman leaned on her broom and gave him a sour look. "I ain't deaf. I can hear ya, boy." Her voice was sharp. "What do you want?"

Tommy lowered the megaphone. "Sorry. We're trying to find my friend's dog."

"She's missing," Victoria added. "A policeman said someone who lived on this corner saw her. Was it you?"

"That was your dog, was it now?" the old woman asked, suspicion in her voice. "Did you give her a reason to run away?"

"Oh no!" Victoria cried. "I love her very much. I take very good care of her. The policeman said another dog was with her. I think she was dog-napped!"

"You do, do you?" the woman said. "Well, I saw her, and the ugly big dog too. I don't think he was a dog. Never saw a dog like that, anyway. Looked more like a wolf, you know."

Olivia glanced at Sandy. Sandy returned her look. *A wolf?* Olivia mouthed, her face going pale.

"Where were they going?" Tommy became impatient to leave.

"Hard to say," the woman snapped at him. "They didn't stop to chat."

"Did you notice which way they ran?" Victoria jumped in with her sweet voice. "We're trying to find Natasha—that's my dog's name—before it gets dark."

"You think that's a good idea, little girl? You children, all alone, following those dogs? The one looked pretty mean." The old lady frowned.

Olivia felt uneasy. She thought the same thing.

"We'll be careful. We promise," Victoria pleaded.

"Just tell us which way they went, please. It means a lot to me."

"Since you're asking nice," the woman said, "they was running toward the highway, going north toward Mount Diablo."

Neither the old woman nor the children paid any attention to a very small bird calling *fee beee, fee beee* right over their heads.

The children got back on their bikes. "Thank you," Victoria called to the old woman. "We'd better be going."

"Don't look like you're going nowhere." The woman pointed to the street. "Now ain't that something."

The children turned their heads, and their eyes opened wide. The street was filled with a huge flock of wild turkeys: Hen turkeys; tom turkeys; and lots of chicks, all going *gobble gobble gobble*.

More than two hundred wild turkeys covered the sidewalks. They crowded onto the lawns. They blocked the corner in both directions.

A car coming down the street braked to a stop and blew its horn. The turkeys didn't move. A man stuck his head out of the car window. His face got very red. He yelled at the birds. A tom turkey stretched out his neck, fanned out his tail feathers, and gobbled angrily. The man beeped the car horn again. The turkeys didn't budge.

The car finally backed up, turned around, and went off the way it had come.

"Can we get through those birds?" Sandy asked.

"Do they bite?" Victoria looked at the turkeys' dark beaks.

"I don't know if they bite," Tommy admitted. "But I bet they kick. The big ones have sharp bony spurs on the back of their legs. We'll have to backtrack just like the car did and make a detour. We can ride a couple of streets down, then come back on the other side. It shouldn't take too long."

"Another bad omen." Sandy shook his head. "We're losing more time." He looked at the sky. The sun sat closer to the horizon. Evening was falling. Dark would come soon. He didn't want to be in the woods when nighttime arrived.

"You're acting like a wimp again, Sandy," Tommy shouted. "Come on, we can ride fast." And the four children, pedaling hard with their backs hunched down over their handlebars, rode their bikes back down the street.

The old woman watched the children until they turned the corner and disappeared from sight. Then she looked at the turkeys, who stopped gobbling and started to move into a line. As if following a signal, they suddenly flapped their large wings. Like a squadron of jet fighters, one after another, they lifted from the ground and flew upward, as high as the rooftops. They turned to the left and took to the open skies, and within a moment they had vanished into the deepening blue. All they left behind as proof that they had been there was a feather, or maybe two.

Back in the junkyard, up on Mount Diablo, Paco and B-Boy waited for the cats to come back. To make the most of the time, they decided to crawl around the edge of the campsite. They wanted to come up behind Natasha and get as close as possible.

Paco realized that being two *small* dogs instead of two bigger ones put them at an advantage. They would be hard to spot, and chances were, if the werewolf did hear any rustling or catch a glimpse of something moving, he would think it was one of the large, hungry junkyard rats. He certainly wouldn't be expecting a rescue party, especially one made up of a Chihuahua, a Jack Russell terrier, and two skinny cats.

Carefully, quietly, the two dogs slunk close to the ground, crawled on their bellies, and made their way toward the spot where Natasha lay. Her head rested on her paws. Her ears folded down. Her eyes squeezed closed. She looked as unhappy as a dog could look.

Paco and B-Boy stopped behind some rusted corrugated roofing not ten feet away from their captured friend. Paco clearly detected her scent now. Its sweet fragrance lifted his spirits. He didn't stop to think that she would be able to smell him too.

But she did. All of a sudden, Natasha's ears stood

tall. Her eyes snapped open. She lifted her nose and sniffed. She twisted her head around and looked right at the spot where B-Boy and Paco hid. A bark of joy came out of her mouth. She leaped to her feet.

Ay, ay, ay, thought Paco. *This isn't good.*

The bark caught the werewolf's attention. A puzzled look crossed over his ugly face. He curled his lip and showed his huge white fangs. He took a step toward Natasha. Paco tensed. He got ready to charge the huge beast. He'd fight, even if he could never win.

All of a sudden came the clear high sound of a meow.

Another meow rang out, this one defiant and taunting. The werewolf's head whipped around. He spotted two cats swishing their tails back and forth at the edge of the clearing.

"Hey, homely looking!" the black cat yelled.

"I'll get you!" the creature growled.

"Bet you couldn't even catch your own mother!" Norma-Jean spat at him. She turned tail and ran as fast as she could, Little Annie at her side. They scooted across an old washing machine. They jumped over a bicycle with only one wheel. They zigged and zagged, going one way, then switching course and going another.

The werewolf roared. He got madder and madder as they outran him. He couldn't catch those two doggone cats, who were—yes, they were—laughing at him.

Not wanting him to give up the chase, Norma-Jean and Little Annie slowed down so that the beast could nearly grab them. When he got very close, they made a beeline for a mud puddle. They easily leaped over it. The werewolf splashed through, getting even dirtier and getting his feet very wet. Now, he made a squishy sound when he ran.

Next, the cats scampered up a huge, gooey mountain of old newspapers and rotting vegetables. They stopped at the very top. "Yoo ooo! Mr. Funny Looking. Where did you learn to run? At a turtle race?"

The werewolf bellowed, "I'll get you! I'll get you right now." He started climbing up the pile of garbage. But his feet were wet. He slipped and slid all the way up the mound. When he reached the top, he took a mighty swipe at the cats with his long arms and razor-sharp claws.

They just giggled and jumped away, heading down the other side of the garbage hill, graceful as gazelles.

The werewolf plunged after them. He didn't realize until it was too late that his wet feet acted like skis, pulling out from under him. "Aiiiiii!" he screamed.

Whack! He fell, coming down hard on the slimy mountain of trash. Suddenly his body acted like a sled on ice. He zoomed out of control down the garbage hill on his back. At the bottom, he smacked into a discarded entertainment center. His feet smashed into the screen of an old TV set.

He pulled himself loose and stood up. He roared. His temper exploded. He thought about nothing but getting hold of those two cats. He'd tear them to pieces. He'd munch on their bones. They'd never laugh at him again.

But they were laughing at him now. Laughing and pointing at a potato peel hanging off one of his ears.

He raced after the cats, going farther and farther from the clearing, toward the row of trees along the white road.

Paco and B-Boy didn't waste a second. They rushed to Natasha's side. Her face brightened with joy, and her eyes filled with tears. "I knew you'd come. I knew you would," she said. "It was all I had to hope for."

"Shhh, shhh. We're here." Paco gave her face a lick on one side, and B-Boy gave her a lick with his little pink tongue on the other side, just to make her feel better.

"Get me loose, please," Natasha pleaded.

"But how?" Paco said. "I didn't bring a knife. Maybe we can chew through the rope."

"There's no time for that," Natasha told them. "I think you can unbuckle my collar, though. You have such small teeth, Paco, I know you can do it. It's my favorite designer suede collar, but I don't care. I just want to go home." A sob choked her, and she couldn't say anything else.

Paco had unbuckled lots of things. He had attacked many a shoe. He had undone several purse straps. He was a professional safecracker when it came to buckles. His lips turned up in a happy grin. He certainly could do it.

"Lie down Natasha, so I can reach it," he told her, and she did.

"Hurry, Paco, hurry!" B-Boy raced around and around the two dogs. His nerves jangled. His feet needed to move. He thought he was going to jump out of his skin.

Paco hurried. He grasped the leather of the collar where it went through the buckle. His teeth were just the right size to do it. He tugged. He pulled. He got the toggle out of the hole in the leather. He pulled again. It was easy for Paco, yes it was. Being a small dog meant he could do things a big dog couldn't. In a few seconds, Natasha's collar fell to the ground. She was free!

She stood up and shook herself. "Thank you, Paco." Her voice rang out like silver bells, music to his ears.

"Okay, let's go!" B-Boy yelled.

"Wait!" Natasha said.

"Wait?" Paco cocked his head to one side as if to ask *why?*

"You two climb on my back and grip my fur in your teeth. I can run faster than you. I am an Afghan hound. My breed can run like the wind. Now come on, get on!" And they did.

Down the winding path through the broken

appliances, past the huge cement culverts, around the piles of pipes, Natasha ran, the two little dogs riding her like jockeys on her back. She ran until she reached the white gravel road. She turned downhill and began to run toward the trees.

All of sudden, they heard a terrible howl. They heard a roar. They heard an angry feline yowl. Actually, they heard two of those.

Then they saw the werewolf, shimmying up a big tree.

Ay, ay, ay, thought Paco. He hadn't planned on the werewolf being able to climb.

The werewolf went higher and higher, up through the foliage, up to where the trunk was very thin.

The two small cats sat perched way out on a tiny branch, at the very tip-top of the tree, where they hoped the werewolf couldn't reach them. But maybe he could. He was getting very high, and his front legs were very long, and his huge claws were very sharp.

"I'm going to dash right past him," Natasha said.

"I can run faster than he can anyway. He's really quite clumsy and slow. Hang on now!"

"*Alto!*" Paco cried.

Natasha halted. "What's wrong?"

Paco let go of her fur and slipped to the ground.

"Paco, what are you doing? He can catch *you*." Natasha looked at him, her eyes filled with concern.

"You go on ahead. Go as far as the highway. If you don't see me coming in a few minutes, start for home. The children are following us, and they may be almost here."

Natasha's whole body stiffened. "The children? Victoria too? Coming here?"

Paco nodded solemnly. "Yes, so go quickly. You need to go."

"But why are you staying?"

"I have to stop the werewolf. And those cats in that tree? Those are my cats, Little Annie and Norma-Jean. I've gotten them into this trouble. I have to get them out of it. They're my family, you see."

Natasha shook her head that yes, she did see. "Take care, my little friend," she whispered, and then, in a great burst of speed, with B-Boy on her back holding on as tightly as he could, she streaked down the road, past the tree where the werewolf climbed, and was gone.

CHAPTER 13

The children were indeed getting closer to the lair of the werewolf. The rain of gull poop had slowed them down. The turkeys had made them take a detour. But even with the delays, they quickly reached the hiking trail that ran along the highway. The path was paved and well kept. They traveled northward at a fast pace. Every now and then, they stopped their bikes and let Victoria use the megaphone to call Natasha's name.

"*Natashaaaaa!*

"*Natashhhaaaa!* Come, girl, Come on!" she cried, her voice echoing through the trees.

No dog answered her call with a bark or a woof or a howl. The children would wait a moment before getting back on their bikes and traveling on.

None of them noticed the small bird with the black cap on the top of her head flying along with them, calling *dee dee dee, dee dee dee.* She sounded like any other chickadee. But she wasn't. She was a chickadee spy.

Pedaling fast, racing the clock, the children were

soon far from town. Each of them, although they didn't say it out loud, felt a bit discouraged. Olivia thought the whole journey was a mistake, and that she would get in trouble when she got home. Sandy worried about the omens and what dangers might lay ahead. Tommy thought that if they didn't find Natasha, he would stop looking like a hero in Victoria's eyes.

Yet Victoria, who became sadder and sadder as they went farther and farther from home, wouldn't give up, not yet. She needed to try. Her Natasha was out there alone. She pleaded with her friends each time they stopped. *Let's go on, just a little longer, oh please.*

And so they did.

In fact, they were very close to Mount Diablo when the bird above them changed her song from *dee dee dee* to a two-note whistle that went *fee beee, fee beee.*

The children, intent on moving ahead, didn't even notice.

Speeding along, wanting to go faster and faster, they rounded a sharp curve—where suddenly they put on their brakes so hard that their bikes skidded. Sandy nearly fell.

Smack-dab in the middle of the path stood two skunks, their backs to the children, their tails raised in battle position. Two more skunks strolled out of the woods. One stopped on the far side of the path, and the other stopped on the near side, keeping anyone from trying to go around the first two skunks. With a gleam in their licorice-colored eyes, they also turned around, raised their tails, and did a little dance up on the toes of their hind feet. All four were ready to attack with their smelly weapons.

"Go back! Push your bikes back!" Tommy yelled to the others.

"They're going to spray!" The children scurried backward and stopped. Their mouths open, their eyes wide, they stared at the four skunks lined up like soldiers in their path.

"What are we going to do now?" Olivia asked. "We can't pass them. They'll get us."

"What are they doing here?" Victoria cried. "Are they rabid? Why are they in the path?"

"It's another omen. It's the third," Sandy explained. He read a lot of books, and he knew about the power of three things. "The third omen is the final warning. We need to go home or something terrible will happen."

"No!" Victoria cried with the saddest of cries and burst into tears.

"But what else can we do, Victoria?" Olivia said gently. "We can't get around the skunks without getting sprayed. And maybe they are rabid. Maybe they will bite us."

"I don't know. I don't know," Victoria sobbed. "But Natasha is out there somewhere. I know she is! I can't leave her!"

Sandy tried to think. Tommy tried to think. Olivia did think.

"Well, you know what?" Olivia's voice was kind. "If you think she's close by, let's stay right here for a while. Use the megaphone and keep calling her. We have a little time. Your voice will carry a long way, and we'll just wait. Will that do?"

Victoria pulled a tissue from her pocket and wiped her nose. Her voice was trembling. "OK. Let's try that. Yes, let's."

So the children got off their bikes. The skunks stayed in the path, but they lowered their tails and turned around. Now they simply sat down, watching the children while Natasha used the bullhorn to call in the saddest of sad voices, *Natashaaaa. Natashhaaa,* over and over again.

CHAPTER 14

Up on the mountain Natasha streaked by the tree that held the two yowling cats and one snarling, fearsome creature. She disappeared with B-Boy into the darkness of the tunnel of trees. Only then did Paco do what he had planned. He gave the victory signal, V in Morse code: three short yips and a long bark. Three short yips and a long bark.

From the very tip-top of the tall tree, the cats responded: "Mew mew mew, Meow!" Then came another plaintive feline call that needed no translation or Morse code. It was "Heeeellllllp!"

When he heard that, something snapped inside of Paco. He didn't hesitate. He didn't feel scared. He took off running toward the tree. He ran fast, faster than he had ever run before, his tail rigid, his small teeth bared, his anger in flames…and when he got to the tree, his momentum carried him straight up the trunk until the creature's fur bottom was right in front of his face.

Paco did the obvious thing: he bit the werewolf—hard—in the hindquarters and held on.

Or, if we tell it the way the story goes in the legend told by the wild creatures from that time forth, the tiny Chihuahua with the big, brave heart bit the monster right in the butt. Paco bit him so hard that the werewolf roared loud enough to shake the ground. Paco bit him so hard that the beast let go of the tree trunk and started to fall.

Paco let go and fell too, rolling over as he hit the ground so he wouldn't be crushed by the huge werewolf. And being light and small and landing on the grass, he came down without a sound and without a scratch.

The werewolf, being big and heavy, hit the rocky road with a crash and a loud grunt. However, also being very hairy, he wasn't hurt. The great beast leaped to his feet, turned his burning red eyes on the little dog, and growled. "I'll get you for that. And I'll eat you when I do."

Paco heard the threat loud and clear, but what he yelled back was—"Run, kitties! I'll catch up."

With that, Paco turned away. He took off toward the junkyard path.

The monster took chase. His heavy footsteps banged against the earth. His fetid breath stank up the air. But he was, as Natasha had noticed, big and clumsy and not very fast—and Paco was running for his life.

Paco plunged deeper into the junkyard, his legs moving like mad.

The werewolf stayed right behind him.

Paco would never give up. But he would soon be tired. His legs were very short. He didn't have much of a chance. He couldn't win a fight with a werewolf—unless he heard the sounds he was waiting to hear.

And then he did.

He heard the buzzing of bees. He heard the thundering of hooves.

Help had arrived.

The little dog scooted toward a large culvert. He dashed inside and slowed down enough to make sure the werewolf had come in too. The cement of the walls echoed every terrible sound. The werewolf snarled and panted. He yelled that he'd catch Paco, eat him up, and suck on his tiny bones.

But words couldn't scare Paco now. He focused on the plan.

He ran out the other end of the culvert. He dashed straight into another, slightly smaller one.

The werewolf came after him. He hunched over and held his head down when he rushed in.

At that point, Paco gathered up all his courage and purposely went slower. Yes, he went slower. He stayed just a few feet in front of the sharpest, biggest, most awful set of claws that ever was. He wanted the monster to believe he could grab him. Paco wanted the werewolf to stop thinking about anything but catching the pesky little Chihuahua. If he did, he would fall for the most brilliant trick Paco had ever devised…

Now, mere inches from the terrible claws of the werewolf, Paco raced out of the far end of the culvert. He burst into an open space in the junkyard.

And there they were.

A large herd of deer stood like a living wall before him. Dozens of hooves pawed the ground. Dozens of antlers lowered and prepared to charge. And in the sky above, a swarm of hornets buzzed. Stingers at the ready, they circled and swooped.

The werewolf emerged from the big cement pipe. He kept his eyes on Paco, who scooted straight ahead. He never saw the hornets diving like fighter planes until it was too late.

Buzzzzzz! Buzzzzzz! Buzzzzzz!

The swarms of hornets struck. And as the werewolf

tried to swat them away, he ran right into the backside of the huffing, snorting deer.

He screamed again. He changed direction, still pawing at the buzzing hornets.

A deer moved in behind him, lifted his hind legs, and kicked. He hit the werewolf with such force that the beast flew through the air and plopped down in front of an old front door, hanging on one hinge from a doorframe. It was shakily propped up like a gate between two massive piles of pipes.

And this door contained something very special, something critical, something that could save them all, something that Paco knew very well: a doggy door—a rubber flap in a frame.

In that doggy door stood Paco. He barked loudly so that the werewolf heard him. The werewolf charged.

Paco waited until he felt the monster's breath on his back. He waited until he felt the air move as the monster reached out to snatch him up with his needle sharp claws. He waited until the very last second before he dove through the doggy door and bounced onto the ground on the far side.

The enraged beast dove too, right into the flap where Paco had disappeared. But being big and clumsy, the werewolf didn't fit through the doggy door. He got stuck, good and stuck.

Wedged in tight, his head and shoulders on one side of the door and his body on the other, the werewolf was trapped. The great monster was unable to get free.

That's when the herd of deer took action. They kicked at the huge pile of pipes. The pipes started to roll down toward the werewolf. *Smack. Whack. Smack.* The pipes began to roll faster toward the werewolf.

The deer sprang out of danger and were safe.

The werewolf was trapped and was not.

Like the walls of Jericho, the piles of pipes came tumbling down. The great lycanthrope—that terrible monster, that ugly werewolf—was no more.

Paco watched. He cheered. He yelled, *"Muchas gracias, mis amigos!"*

But the deer and the hornets were already gone, melting away into the soft gray of evening.

Now, Paco needed to find his way back to the road. He needed to find his cats and get away from this place of broken things. He needed to return to where everything was whole and good and filled with love. He needed to go home.

Toward the end of the crooked path, toward the white way of the rocky road, toward the tunnel of trees, Paco ran. And there, at the bottom of the tall tree where they had perched on the very smallest branch at the tip-top, sat Little Annie and Norma-Jean.

Paco skidded to a halt. His pink tongue hung

out. His breath was short. "I told you"—*puff, puff*—"to run!"

"We know," they said together. "But we were waiting to see if you needed to be rescued."

"Rescued? Me?" Paco sputtered between puffs. "I just rescued you!"

"We know. But we waited, just in case. Sometimes your plans don't always work out the way they should."

"They did this time, though," Norma-Jean added with a smile. "So let's go home!"

With a cat on either side to guide him through the murky dimness of the tunnel of trees, Paco trotted down the road. He was tired now and trying not to think of the long journey that stretched ahead. He and the cats did have very short legs. The way home would take them a very long time.

Except that, as it turned out, this time it wouldn't.

Once the two cats and the little dog came through the tunnel of trees into the light, they saw a welcome sight. Natasha and B-Boy were coming back up the road to look for them.

"I told you to run!" Paco called out, a little exasperated because nobody listened to him, but awfully happy to see his friends.

"We did," Natasha said. "When you didn't follow, we came back. Friends don't leave friends in trouble. You showed me that. So climb on." And she knelt down on the white stone road.

"Us too?" asked Norma-Jean and Little Annie.

"Why, yes! You saved my life. You're not much bigger than Paco. Even with four friends on my back, I can run like the wind."

So two cats and two dogs got on Natasha's back. They clung tightly to her fur. Then she began to race down Mount Diablo toward the ribbon of white highway stretching southward toward town. Yet when Natasha reached the fork in the road, where the west road went west and the east one they were on met it, she slowed. Her ears perked up. She stopped.

"What's wrong?" asked B-Boy, who rode up front and could see best.

"The highway is straight ahead," Paco called from the back.

"I hear something. Shhhh," Natasha said.

Eight ears perked up and listened too.

"I hear it!" said B-Boy.

"Me too," said Paco.

"Us too," chorused Little Annie and Norma-Jean.

With a bark of joy, Natasha left the fork in the road. She didn't go straight ahead toward the interstate, but dashed right for a paved hiking path Paco had never seen before.

As she barked loudly, nonstop, Natasha's long hound legs ate up the ground with ease. Her golden coat streamed out behind her. Her passengers hung on for dear life. And the Afghan hound ran like the wind.

Not very far away on that very path, but too far off to hear a dog barking, Olivia was saying, "It's really late. Natasha isn't coming. We need to go. I'm sorry, Victoria."

With a heart of stone, Victoria lowered her megaphone. "I know." Her tears rolled down, leaving wet streaks on her cheeks, which were no longer pink as cherries. They were pale and white and smudged with dirt.

Sad and weary, the children went to their bikes, picked them up, and turned them toward home. They were just about to push off, when a small gray bird with a black cap on her head screamed *fee beee, fee beee.*

Suddenly, the four skunks, who had been sitting on the path toward the mountain, now appeared as if by magic on the path toward home. They didn't have their tails up. They didn't hiss or growl. They just stood there.

"What's going on?" Tommy asked out loud.

"It's another bad omen!" moaned Sandy, not remembering that some omens are good ones.

"No!" insisted Olivia. "They're trying to tell us something."

At that very moment, with folded wings and a rush of air, the chickadee swooped down, skimmed across the top of Victoria's long hair, and picked up a strand in her beak. She tugged.

"Ow! Stop that," cried Victoria.

"Turn around," Olivia yelled at her friend. "She's trying to turn you around."

So Victoria did, and the bird let go. From off in the distance she heard a familiar sound. A bark. Then another. And another.

"Natasha!" she screamed. She dropped her bike to the ground and raced up the path. The other children put down their bikes and began to follow, although they didn't catch up right away. The little girl ran so quickly her feet barely touched the ground.

Suddenly, right there in front of them all, coming around a bend was a golden dog, barking madly with a wild joy and rushing into Victoria's open arms. The little girl grasped her beloved dog's neck and buried her face in the huge hound's fur. They stayed there together not moving, Natasha still barking, and Victoria still crying, but crying tears of happiness this time.

In a moment, the other children were there too, with Tommy Thompson out in front, as usual.

He couldn't believe what he saw.

"B-Boy? B-Boy! What you doing here?" He snatched the Jack Russell from Natasha's back and held him up. "It is you, isn't it?"

B-Boy barked yes because it was him, of course.

Then Sandy and Olivia skidded to a halt next to Tommy. Olivia's eyes grew huge and wide. "Paco? Little Annie? Norma-Jean? All my animals are here too." Her mind couldn't make sense of what her eyes saw. "I—I—can't understand this. What's going on?"

It was then that Victoria raised her head from the fur of Natasha's neck and turned to them. She smiled a lovely smile, one that Olivia would never forget.

"I know what's going on. The animals went looking for Natasha. They found her, you see. And brought her back to me. She needed their help, and they gave it. That's what friends do. That's what you have done for me."

EPILOGUE...

OR WHAT HAPPENED NEXT

Bright sun sparkled on blue pool water as Paco unrolled his beach towel next to Coco's. It was Saturday. He and Olivia were at Sandy's for a play date. He plopped himself down next to the chocolate Lab.

Coco had a contented smile on her face. Her white funnel collar was gone. She wore her World's Greatest Dog medal with pride. Her leg felt much better. The stitches were coming out on Monday. She yawned a big yawn. She turned toward her friend.

Paco looked simply smashing. While all the dogs and the two cats snoozed through the day before, worn out by their great adventure, Olivia had gone to the mall. She'd bought a yellow French terry hoodie for Paco that said on its back, "My dog is an angel."

Coco admired Paco's new shirt. "You are an angel," she told him. "And a very brave dog too."

"*Muchas gracias,* Coco. You're making me blush." He couldn't stop grinning at what she said.

"It's all true," broke in Natasha, who lay regally under the beach umbrella. She had spent the day before at the groomer, getting the tangles out of her long coat. Now she glistened like spun gold. "You've the heart of a lion, and not a dandelion either."

"You're the bomb!" yelled B-Boy, as he popped and locked his way backward toward the edge of the pool. Then he did a backflip into the water. Natasha watched him with a smile on her face. She really did like B-Boy. He was quite a dancer.

Paco noticed Natasha's fond gaze following B-Boy and didn't mind. He had his Coco, and she was the one he wanted most. Besides, they were all good friends, so being jealous was just plain...well, plain *dumb*. They were all together. They were all OK. That's what really mattered.

And none of the children had gotten in any trouble when they had returned two nights ago—except for Tommy Thompson. They all made it back home before dark, except for him.

However, being late wasn't even his fault—this time. He rode all the way to Victoria's house with her to make sure she got inside safely. He waited outside until he heard her yell, "Mumsy! Poppy! Natasha just came home!" He heard her parents' cries of joy. Victoria never told them *how* Natasha just came home, and that worked out just fine. There was soon ice cream for everyone, especially the Afghan hound, and laughter served all around.

But Tommy missed his curfew for the second

time in two days. His parents took his bike away for a whole week. He pretended to be upset, but he really wasn't. He kept remembering Victoria's smiles, and the way she looked at him. He could live without his bike for a few days. He was walking on air instead.

Now the boys and girls gathered at Sandy's with their dogs. They all wore their bathing suits. They intended to swim and celebrate Natasha's return. Sandy's dad ordered a pizza and cut up some fruit too. They sat at a table and played Uno for a while. They didn't talk about what had happened the other night. They didn't have to, because they knew.

Well, they knew some of it. They didn't know everything.

"Coco," Paco said, a hint of worry in his voice.

"What, Paco?"

"I told you what I did. Up there in the junkyard. I got thirsty, and I drank rainwater from that footprint."

"Yes, you did."

"Last night, the moon was full. I was *muy* scared. But I didn't change at all. I didn't start to become a werewolf. Nothing happened. Do you think something will tonight?"

"I don't know, Paco. But I rather suspect it won't."

"*Por qué?*"

"Because you can't believe everything you read on the Internet, especially when it comes to magic and charms and ways to turn into a werewolf." She gave him a wise and knowing smile.

Lines formed a furrow on Paco's tiny forehead. "*Sí.* I hope you're right. I don't want to look like that big hairy beast. I like being small. It has its advantages. But what if I do change, Coco? What then?"

Coco's voice got stern. "You listen to me, Paco. Because I am your friend. If you do change on the outside, it won't matter. You'll still be Paco inside, the bravest Chihuahua in the world. You'll still be *you* where it counts. In your heart."

"*Sí. Claro.*" Paco knew what she said was true. So he snuggled close to Coco, who thought he was perfect just the way he was. He closed his eyes, sighed a happy sigh, and took a nap.

ACKNOWLEDGMENTS

Writing is, most of the time, a solitary occupation, carried on with a computer and in a room, with or without a view. But a writer also needs people to come along on her creative journey—for support and encouragement and company when a good cup of tea and sympathy are needed.

Therefore, I would like to thank my long-time agent, John Talbot of the Talbot Fortune Agency, who has been traveling with me since the very beginning. He always reminds me that a writing career is not a sprint, it's a marathon.

I would also like to thank those wonderful early readers who believed in *Chihuawolf* from my very first draft: Priscilla Adams, Frank Bittinger, Hildy Morgan, and Ken Spence. Last, a tip of the hat to Roger Samuels for naming my real-life skunk visitor, Professor Pewmount, which was the perfect name for Paco's wise old friend.

ABOUT THE AUTHOR

Charlee Ganny lives in a 150-year-old farmhouse high on a hill near Harveys Lake, Pennsylvania. She has three dogs, too many cats to count, and lots of visiting wild creatures, including a skunk named Professor Pewmount.

Chihuawolf is her first book for children. She has written nine adult novels. Under the pseudonym Lucy Finn, she writes romantic comedy. As Savannah Russe, she created a *USA Today* bestselling vampire series. She is also a back-of-the-book indexer, and in 2006 she won the American Society for Indexing's H. W. Wilson Award for Excellence in Indexing for her index of Joseph Campbell's *A Skeleton Key to Finnegans Wake: Unlocking James Joyce's Masterwork*.

But most of all, she is a writer and a dreamer, and what she dreams…she writes.